STAIRWAY
TO
HELL!

Murphy

Hawke surged up the stairs. Two weapons fired from above: the gunmen were expecting him to continue. He dug out another grenade, pulled the safety pin, and edged upward. He saw an office setup. Behind a desk he spotted two gunmen. He rolled the grenade under the desk. It stopped when it hit a brown pants leg and exploded.

One more floor. Hawke rammed through double doors and up the steps toward six, and as he did he saw ten gang members running toward him. He fired the Spas-12 four times and the men flopped to the ground in various stages of agony and death. Behind them a door closed. Hawke backed up and fired two rounds, and the hot lead blew away the thin metal door jamb.

Someone fired a handgun twice, but Hawke was already standing against the wall and out of the line of bullets.

"Who the hell are you?" a voice called from inside the room.

"An avenging angel—who's here to collect!"

The Book Rack
A Paperback Exchange
3217 E. State Blvd.
202 Southgate Plaza
Fort Wayne, Indiana

$1.75

T5-AFS-413

Also by Chet Cunningham

THE AVENGER

THE AVENGER #2:
HOUSTON HELLGROUND

THE AVENGER #3:
COLOMBIAN CRACKDOWN

**Published by
WARNER BOOKS**

ATTENTION: SCHOOLS AND CORPORATIONS

WARNER books are available at quantity discounts with bulk
purchase for educational, business, or sales promotional use For
information, please write to: SPECIAL SALES DEPARTMENT,
WARNER BOOKS, 666 FIFTH AVENUE, NEW YORK, N.Y. 10103.

ARE THERE WARNER BOOKS
YOU WANT BUT CANNOT FIND IN YOUR LOCAL STORES?

You can get any WARNER BOOKS title in print. Simply send title
and retail price, plus 50c per order and 50c per copy to cover
mailing and handling costs for each book desired. New York State
and California residents add applicable sales tax. Enclose check
or money order only, no cash please, to: WARNER BOOKS, P.O.
BOX 690, NEW YORK, N.Y. 10019.

THE Avenger #4

Chet Cunningham

MANHATTAN MASSACRE

WARNER BOOKS

A Warner Communications Company

WARNER BOOKS EDITION

Copyright © 1988 by Chet Cunningham
All rights reserved.

Warner Books, Inc.
666 Fifth Avenue
New York, N.Y. 10103

 A Warner Communications Company

Printed in the United States of America

First Printing: October, 1988

10 9 8 7 6 5 4 3 2 1

CHAPTER
ONE

Shensi stirred where she lay in the alley down from Pell Street and stared with only partly open eyes at the filth, the human waste, the litter and trash of a thousand Chinese that lay around her in the Manhattan dawn. The acrid stench of urine hung in the air. She was just past fifteen, with long, matted black hair, and dark brown eyes in a face shrunken and pale. She touched a bruise on one cheek with dirty fingers and stared at her broken nails.

Shensi looked over at the girl who shared with her half a blanket and surveyed the cramped space behind a garbage dumpster where they had slept last night.

Shensi wore only a thin skirt and blouse, and she shivered in the chill of the early September morning. She rubbed her watery eyes, then sniffed and gently pushed the shoulder of the girl beside her. There was no reaction. She frowned, her Chinese features becoming sharp and her eyes alert.

When Shensi pushed the girl again, her whole body moved. Shensi touched the girl's forehead. It was cold and her eyes stared at the dumpster without seeing it. There was no life left in the slender figure of Shensi's last friend in the whole world.

Shensi wanted to cry for the girl, but she had cried herself out a year ago. Crying didn't help you survive down here. And she *would* survive!

Shensi sat up, looked for her shoes, then remembered that someone had stolen them last night.

For a moment she stared at the line of tracks up and down both arms. Similar marks punctured both her legs and her sides, wherever she could reach. She was hurting for a fix. Shensi had no friends to go to. Most of them were broke, in jail, or dead.

A fuzzy, half-remembered pleasant thought came to her. Then it slid away. She had to get it back. It was a plan, a way to get out of this stink hole, a way to get a fix whenever she needed it! The young guy had said if all else failed, this place would be glad to help her.

What the hell was it? Some damned do-gooders?

It came back to her in bits and pieces. A man, on the corner of Pell and Mott. Easy. He wore nice clothes, he was clean, looked straight. But he said he could help. He hadn't minded talking to her even though she was a wreck looking for a fix. He had said this place might be a real chance for her.

Yes! one last chance. Something about a palace. Oh yes! she would like to live in a palace! She tried to make her pained, drug-clouded mind function. Her head spun. Her gut felt as if somebody were twisting a hot iron inside it. She tried to think.

Some of it came back. The man had called it the Palace of Radiance and Beauty. Yes! that was it. He said it was a Garden of Mystical Pleasures. She concentrated until her head pounded. What else had he said? Slowly more came. There all her troubles would be washed away, all her problems shed, every worry smashed, and every desire she ever had satisfied!

She had to find him!

She had nothing else. No man would pay her to lay on her back in the alley with him. She had no money, no friends, no room, no clothes to sell, no radio or TV to hock.

Yes, she knew there would be a price. With a clean, well dressed guy like him, it would be a terrible price. But what did it matter to her now? She had nothing to lose. Triad? Probably. Maybe he wanted her for a house? No, he could get all the girls for that he wanted. Another term came but she didn't even know what it meant—New Control. She had heard it somewhere. Hell, so what? There was a high price just for living. She had to get to the corner of Pell and Mott streets.

Shensi spent a great deal of her remaining energy and concentration trying to stand. She got up to her knees and leaned against the brick wall, but as she stretched up she lost her balance and fell on the dead girl.

"Sorry," she said, and tried again. This time she got to one knee and placed one foot under her before her head spun around and she toppled against the dumpster, then back down onto the alley. She brushed dried dog droppings off her blouse and tried again.

She made it. She pushed away from the nearby brick wall and, steadying herself against it and the dumpster, stepped over the dead girl. For a moment she looked down. Shensi couldn't even remember the girl's name. Billy? Barbara? She was fourteen. "Sorry," she said, and took a step up the alley.

At the end of the garbage bin she looked out cautiously. She saw only a few more street people in the alley, some still sleeping or too sick to move, some sleeping under cardboard. One older man clutched a new blanket around him and glared at her. She avoided them all and walked with great care in the morning haze of Manhattan toward Pell Street and the key. She had to find the magic key that would let her enter the Palace of Radiance and Beauty.

It took her a half hour to work over to Pell and then down four blocks to Mott Street, her slow pace a contrast to the early morning bustle of New York City's Chinatown. She paused to rest against the wall of the Temple Garden. She could make it, she thought. She had to.

She realized for a moment that her appearance was not right for this busy street, but she moved on and at last found Mott. The slick young man had been on this side just a few nights ago. Or had it been a few weeks? Her mind played tricks on her. No food and no fix did that to her. She closed her eyes and leaned against the street-lamp standard.

She would have vomited but there was nothing in her stomach. She didn't have the strength to dry-heave. Her eyes drifted shut and she almost fell.

She saw a middle-aged Chinese man watching her. He moved on, shaking his head and smoothing down the vest of his suit.

She waited for an hour, then two hours, but she did not see the man she hunted. At last she sat down against the front wall of the Gourmet Village restaurant. The owner came out and screamed at her in Chinese to move on, but she ignored him.

An hour later someone squatted beside her.

"Shensi, remember me? Were you looking for me?"

She turned her head with an effort and saw the same young Chinese man with the fresh blue suit, nice tie, and clean-shaven face. He was the one she had talked to before.

"The Palace of Radiance and Beauty," she mumbled.

"You want to go there and forget your troubles?"

"Yes, no troubles." She was having difficulty keeping him in focus. She shook her head. "A fix whenever I need one."

"It's yours. Are you ready?"

Shensi nodded, her eyes fell shut, and she slumped forward unconscious in his arms. The young Chinese smiled.

"I will take good care of you, small lotus blossom. You indeed will find radiance and beauty."

He carried her into the Chinese herb store beside the restaurant, through to the back room, and then to the alley. There he went down four doors and knocked on one that had no name on it.

It opened. An equally sharp looking young Chinese youth looked out, nodded, and carried Shensi into a small room. There were steps directly ahead. He went down them a flight, along a narrow hallway, and then down steps again.

It was two hours before Shensi awoke. She came back to reality with a jolt and saw the hypodermic needle coming out of her arm. Someone pulled free the rubber tube that had bound her upper arm. For a moment she wanted to scream. Then she smiled and felt the immediate flood of vitality and strength that flowed through her. She tried to hug the woman who had given her the shot.

"Now we make you beautiful," the Chinese woman said. She was far from beautiful herself—short, heavy, with coarse features and straight black hair cut close around a stern face.

The shot gave Shensi more energy than she could remember. It must be good shit, maybe even China White! Eagerly she helped as much as she could as the older woman gave her a hot tub bath and washed her hair.

The bath was beautiful! She luxuriated in the hot water. It had been so long since she had really washed her hands and face. Years it seemed since an honest-to-God bath!

Then there was food that even tasted good and some wine. At last she lay on a soft couch while another woman— this one small, slender, and pretty—picked out clothes for her.

Shensi studied herself in a mirror. "Am I to look like a princess?" she asked shyly. "I've never had clothes like those before." The small woman looked up and frowned for a moment, then blinked quickly and turned away. When she looked back she said nothing.

Shensi wondered about the Palace of Radiance and Beauty. "Is this it? Is this the Palace?" she asked. The woman nodded curtly and went on combing out the tangles in her shoulder-length hair. When her hair came free of snarls, the woman brushed it until it shone in the lights.

They helped her put on her new clothes. Strangely, no undergarments, but she had not owned any for almost a year now anyway. The gown was low cut, revealing, but of fine silk, and it felt delicious against her skin. Soon another woman came in, much younger, who talked a steady stream, but Shensi understood little of what she said. This girl applied makeup to Shensi, covering up the bruise on her cheek and lightening the sunken look of her eyes. When Shensi glanced in a mirror she did not recognize herself.

"What a beautiful girl!" she said, then giggled. Her headache was coming back. She needed anther jolt.

"I need another pop," she told the talkative Chinese girl. "Just a quick one."

The girl smiled. "First you must write a letter."

"Letter, I don't understand."

"You must write the letter. How do you think you're paying for all of this?"

When she still didn't understand, the other girl shrugged and walked out of the room. Shensi tried the knob and found the door locked. She knocked.

At once it opened and the man from the street stepped in. He was dressed as before. He had a pad of cheap newsprint paper and a ballpoint pen.

"It's time to write the note," he said. "You can call me Willy." He led her to a small table and chair at the side of the room and helped her sit down.

"I need another jolt of that joy juice," she pleaded.

Willy showed her the filled hypodermic in his pocket. "Just as soon as you write the letter."

"What letter?" she asked.

"The letter we talked about—don't you remember?"

"No."

"A note to your brother telling him how hard it is on the street. Just a short note."

She frowned, then looked at the fix. "I can do that."

She sat down, took the pen, and wrote a line, then a second one. Willy read over her shoulder.

"Yes, good. How about saying life isn't worth living in the Chinatown gutters."

She wrote it.

"Maybe you could say there's only one way to find peace."

She looked up at him, shrugged, and wrote it.

"Now sign it with your whole name, first and last."

With a clearly read hand, she wrote, Shensi Wong.

Willy took the paper, read it, folded it twice, and put it in his suit coat pocket. He placed the rubber tube around her left arm, let the vein pop up, and gave her the shot. She hugged him.

He left and two more women came in. One carried the most beautiful gown she had ever seen. It was of fine lace and had six flouncy petticoats, and when she put it on, it was cut so low that it showed almost all of her breasts. But they told her it was exactly right for the party she was going to.

"A party? I haven't been to a party for a long time."

They put high-heeled shoes on her; then one woman fixed her hair, fluffing it, curling it, and setting it high on her head. Then she let it fall down to one side in a glorious dark rain. When Shensi looked in the mirror she gasped.

"Is this really me?" she asked the woman. The hairdresser could only nod, then quickly left the room.

Willy came in and clapped. "You are beautiful, you are dazzling, I'd like to make love to you right now!" He stepped up to her and kissed her cheek, then fondled her

almost bare breasts a moment. She was so surprised she
didn't react until he stepped back.

"What does all this cost me? I have to fuck a whole triad
or something?"

"Not at all. Come down to my office and I'll explain a
few things to you."

Willy's small office had a big TV set on the desk with a
videotape player on top.

"Sit down; we have a drink for you. It's delicious. I'll
have one too as we talk. We even have a TV video for you
to watch. I have a lot of things to explain to you."

An hour later they came out of the office and the sparkle
had left Shensi's eyes. She walked with Willy along the
hallway and down one more flight of steps into the third
subbasement level. There they entered a room finely furnished
in the style of old China. Here were varnished woods,
pictures by the Chinese masters, and carved ivory figures.
In the center of the forty-foot-long room stood a large,
expensive table. Thirty massive carved chairs sat waiting.

At the sides of the room were a dozen or more small
tables where well-dressed Chinese men gambled. There
were all the Chinese gambling games as well as mah-jongg,
poker, craps, and a roulette wheel.

As soon as Willy and Shensi entered the room, a small
gong sounded and all talk stopped. The men, perhaps forty
or fifty, stood at once and bowed toward Shensi. She gave a
short bow in return and waited.

The men began to walk by her. Most were older than her
father. They kissed her cheek, most of them fondled her
breasts, then moved and sat at the large table.

When the last of the men had come past, a throne chair
carried by four youths wearing only short trunks came in.
She sat on the gold-threaded cushion in the elegantly decorated throne chair and was lifted and carried to the table.

The gamblers all clapped as she sat there regally, watching
them. Harry Han, the one man in the room dressed Chinese

style, stepped forward to the edge of the table and handed her an envelope. She looked in it and found ten one-hundred-dollar bills. She gasped. It was more money than she had ever seen in her life!

Now a gambling cloth of dark green had been spread on the table. She took the envelope and dropped it on the Chinese symbol that meant "no."

The only other bet was "yes."

As soon as her envelope dropped, the men crowded around the betting green, chattering in Chinese, calling to one another. Now the head man, Harry Han, put down a new cloth. The odds on the "yes" side were six to one. On the "no" side it was one to one.

For ten minutes the men talked, argued, watched the girl on the throne chair, and at last all bets were down.

Shensi watched it all in a fuzzy daze. Harry Han clapped three times and those eligible for the front row seats sat down; others stood behind them and waited. Harry reached in a drawer in the large table, took out a silver box, and put it on the table.

He opened the box and removed a chrome plated .38 caliber revolver with a four-inch barrel. From a box he took out one silver cartridge. He opened the cylinder and held it up so all could see that there were no rounds in it. Then in plain sight and with no sleight of hand, he pushed the round into the revolver's cylinder and closed it.

At once he leaned forward and handed the weapon to Shensi. Her eyes glowed with fury. She was going to win the game! She knew she would. The girl in the video had won! She took the weapon in her hands. She had never held a firearm before. She had been instructed exactly what to do next.

She looked down at her envelope on the "no" side of the betting cloth. If she won her bet, she would have two thousand dollars and could buy all the heroin she needed!

Shensi swallowed. Her drug-clouded mind was starting to

clear, but now it was too late. She had accepted the China White, she had let them bathe and dress and make her beautiful in the Palace of Radiance and Beauty.

She lifted the weapon and pushed down halfway on the cylinder lock, then spun the cylinder the way Willy had taught her. The cylinder turned around and around and stopped.

Shensi looked at the chrome plated weapon. Was she holding her own death in her hands? Was there anything she could do about it? Willy had told her about the girl who had done everything right, then at the last second aimed the weapon at one of the men and pulled the trigger.

The bettor had died and she had too, but only after four days of the most painful kind of torture the experts could devise.

Shensi took a deep breath. All talk around the table had stopped. She lifted the weapon, then shook her head and spun the cylinder again. The odds were with her. Six to one that she would win! This time when the rotation of the cylinder came to a stop, she lifted the weapon with her right hand, put her finger on the trigger, and, before she could think about it, pulled.

In the split second before the hammer fell, Harry Han felt a surge of emotion, the way he did every time. His hips bucked as he climaxed where he stood at the side of the room.

The revolver's hammer fell and hit the .38 caliber silver shell, exploding the primer and the powder charge.

It was the merest blink in the eye of eternity as the silver bullet spun out of the short barrel, jolted into Shensi's right temple, penetrated her brain and came out her forehead spraying those on that side of the table with her blood, fragments of her skull, and a shower of soft white and pink brain tissue.

The cooling body that had once been Shensi Wong flopped against the side of the throne chair. The four young men ran forward, picked up the long poles under the throne chair, lifted it high over the heads of the Chinese men who crowded around the betting side of table shouting and screeching for their six-to-one payoff. The chair vanished quickly out double doors at the end of the room.

Harry Han called in his clerk, who lined the men up and quietly paid each his six-to-one odds. Harry had collected the money from the "no" bets and to one side he counted it. Over eighty-five thousand dollars. Not nearly enough to cover the six-to-one bets on the other side of the board. But the thrill of the sideshow brought in the gamblers.

It was advertising. Anyone could build and maintain a gambling hall for Chinese only. But his was the only one that had this special attraction. Where else could you bet on a human life, a live or die situation? He had to turn away dozens of gamblers every night and had jumped his buy-in to ten thousand at the door.

Harry laughed softly as he watched the bettors. Over the course of the evening he would be well ahead. His total profits just kept going up and up.

The throne chair carriers, having moved the chair and body out of the gambling room, set the chair down at the end of the next room and ran out a side door. A tall, thin Chinese man watched them with scorn. He had only one eye but didn't wear a patch. His face was distorted where a .22 round had blasted through the side of his head and out of his left eye. He had refused plastic surgery. He looked at his face every day; others could as well.

He lifted the corpse from the throne chair and carried it through another door. There he carefully removed the expensive gown. It would have to be cleaned before it was used again. He lay the naked girl on the stainless steel table and made a phone call.

A woman came in shortly and took the dress without looking at the girl. It was the same woman who had dressed her only a few hours before.

The one-eyed man checked the girl again. What a waste of a beautiful child. She was no more than sixteen. He knew bodies. Quickly and with professional skill, he removed all of the makeup from the girl's face. Then he washed her face three times with a strong alcohol-based cleaner to take off every trace of the makeup that had penetrated her skin.

He used remover to detach the false fingernails from her own broken nails and then washed them as well with the alcohol solution.

At last he looked at her naked body, stark, lifeless, and pale. He nodded. From a drawer in his stainless steel undertaker's table, he took out a box and opened it. From the box he lifted handfuls of dirt, oiled sawdust, and other debris from an alley halfway across town and rubbed it into the girl's hands, arms, feet, and partway up her legs.

He caked it in her hair, rubbed it in her scalp. He paid special attention to her face, leaving the long bruise exposed but making her face appear as grimy as when she first entered the Palace of Radiance and Beauty.

The undertaker checked his watch. She had been dead for an hour. Lots of time yet before her body stiffened. Her blood would show plenty of drugs for the autopsy. He had left the bullet wound untouched.

The woman who had taken away the fancy ball gown came back with the clothes Shensi had been wearing when Willy brought her in. The thickest Chinese woman quickly put the blouse and skirt on the girl. She handed a much folded sheet of newsprint to the tall, thin man with one eye. He opened it and read it, then folded it again and pushed it inside the girl's blouse; he made sure her blouse was tucked inside her skirt so the suicide note would stay close to her body. The woman watched, then left without a word.

Then he made a phone call and left the room. Two Chinese street toughs came in, stared at the girl, made obscene remarks, then wrapped a grimy blanket around her and carried her out a side door into an alley.

A small pickup truck had been backed up to the door. All that was left of Shensi was dropped into the truck. One kid stayed in back as the other drove.

Eight blocks over, in the edge of Chinatown, the kid in back wrapped the body tightly with the blanket and dropped it in an alley as the pickup kept moving.

An hour later, just before it started to get dark, a Manhattan NYPD prowl car stopped in the alley, and the second man in the car checked the blanket.

"Yeah," the Irish rookie cop said,, looking at his partner in the car. "We've got a DB here. Chinese girl, teenager I'd guess, but it's hard to tell."

The driver called it in and they waited for Homicide. They had been almost off shift. Now they would be tied up for two hours doing the paperwork.

A day later Matt Hawke read the story again in the *New York Daily News*. They had splashed it over the front page for two days. They duly reported the suicide note and showed photos of six more similar notes. All had been found on Chinese girls in Chinatown; all the girls had been shot in the head with one round. The wording of the last two lines of each note was similar enough to be suspicious.

The newspaper made some wild speculation about how the girls died. It said all of the last six girls had been junkies, and all had nonlethal amounts of heroin in their systems when they died. Hawke read on and at last found what he needed, the names of survivors: a brother, David, who was a loan officer at the highly respected Chinese First American Bank in Chinatown, and a sister, Jasmine, an actress and dancer.

At five-thirty that afternoon, Hawke met the man a bank clerk had earlier identified as David Wong as he came out the employees' entrance of the bank.

"David Wong, I want to talk to you about your sister. Don't even turn around, just keep walking up the block and go into the next store. I'm not with the police or with the Mafia or the Chinese triads. I want to find out who killed her.''

David Wong swung around. "Killed her? You don't think it was suicide?''

"No, and neither do you. But I need your help to get much farther into the Chinese community here.''

"Why do you say she was killed?''

"The similarity of more than a dozen other such deaths. Most junkies don't have the guts to kill themselves with a gun. An OD would be more likely. These dozen deaths have all been Chinese. Isn't that strange, with Chinese a tiny minority of the twelve million people in town?''

David Wong was twenty-six years old, about five-ten, lean and trim. He looked like a long distance runner. His business suit, while not new, was clean and pressed. His face worked for a moment.

"If what you say is true, should we be talking this way?''

"No, so turn around and I'll be behind you. I have a car a block up the street.''

A few minutes later they got in the rented Ford Mustang, drove over to the East River, and parked.

"Mr. Wong. My name is Matt Hawke. I'm here investigating the Chinese connection, the takeover by Chinese criminals of the heroin trade in New York City's five boroughs. For several years I worked with the Drug Enforcement Administration. Then my wife was killed in San Diego by drug dealers, and I quit the agency to go after drug criminals on my own.

"I use their own money to fight them. Right now I'm working on a group called the New Control.''

As Hawke said the name he saw David Wong stiffen.

"You've heard of this group?''

"Yes. Everyone in Chinatown knows of it . . . and if they are honest, they fear it. Many of the law-abiding people in this community fear that the New Control will develop into an organization as powerful and as criminal as the Italian Mafia.''

''That's why I need your assistance.''

''I don't see how I can be any help. I'm a banker. I don't even know anyone in the triads, let alone the New Control.''

''I think your sister's murder may be a wedge we can use to break into that New Control. There's a pattern here; what we have to do is put the pattern together and see where it leads, then I'll follow it.''

David Wong shook his head. ''No offense, Mr. Hawke, but you couldn't even get into a minor tong's Wednesday night poker party. How do you expect...''

''I hope that you'll help me, Mr. Wong. I'd have a hard time infiltrating down here.''

David Wong stared out the window. He rubbed his eyes a moment and then looked at Hawke. ''Yes, I'll help. I knew that Shensi was on drugs. She was only fifteen. Our parents are dead, and I was trying to hold the family together. She rebelled two years ago and ran away. I found her once. She was on the street as a hooker to pay for the drugs she needed. At fifteen! I took her home and she ran away again when I wouldn't get heroin for her. She was a slave to it. I...I had to identify her body two days ago. Her funeral was yesterday.''

''You don't have to tell your other sister about this,'' Hawke said. ''We won't involve her. I need you to do some quiet investigation, nothing dangerous. Maybe help me get into a few places I couldn't go by myself. Call me a drunken client, something like that.''

''I don't know. This could get me killed. These people, these Chinese gangsters, aren't like the Mafia, you know. They are not as well organized. There are probably ten or twelve groups in Manhattan alone, trying to gain control. I have a buddy who is in the DEA. He's plainclothes, and naturally he works Chinatown. The stories he can tell.''

''Right now I wish I was Chinese.''

David Wong looked at him and chuckled. "Afraid that would be a problem." He looked out at the East River. "I owe them. Goddammit, I owe them for what they did to Shensi. Yes! I'll help you. I'll give you my home phone and business phone. Neither one is tapped."

Hawke held out his hand. "Thanks. Without some help I'd have a damn hard time doing any good down here."

"Okay—first, what do you know about the Chinese crime scene in our beloved Chinatown?"

"Very little."

"For starters my DEA friend tells me that Chinese organized crime groups are the number one emerging danger in New York City, not just regarding drugs, but extortion, gambling, and prostitution as well.

"Right now the police think that the Chinese Connection runs at least seventy percent of the heroin into the five boroughs. The Mafia is the big loser on the competition here.

"My DEA friend says the Chinese are following an old American custom. The Irish immigrants had a crime core in decades past; so did the Jews and the Italians. With each wave of immigrants there was a small nucleus of criminals who first preyed on their countrymen, then moved out to hit society as a whole. The same thing is now happening with the Chinese community.

"Youth gangs are a big problem. Some of the organized crime groups, and especially the New Control outfit, are big users of gangs. Along the same line, there are a lot of Chinese girls brought into the country illegally every few months to stock Chinese whorehouses in New York and across the country. That's not our concern here, but it could be a factor. Why wasn't Shensi put in one of the houses? She was pretty enough, and only fifteen.

"Oh, something else. For Chinese, the numbers three, six, and eight are lucky. Extortion payments by merchants are often in those amounts—three hundred thirty-three dollars, or six hundred sixty-six, or eight eighty-eight in a 'red envelope' to start. The number four is unlucky and often represents death. Watch out for number four.

"The triads are old, old criminal societies that are now based in Hong Kong and Taiwan. They go back hundreds, maybe thousands, of years and now are powerful in all parts of the world that have many Chinese. If you hear about Red Sticks, watch out. They are the enforcers of the Chinese mob. They beat up folks and kill people. I'll never lend money to any of them."

Hawke looked up to find David Wong grinning.

"So, my new friend, just where the hell do we start?"

CHAPTER
TWO

Hawke watched David Wong evaluating him, dissecting his every expression, every move. He was grieving, but he was still absolutely determined to avenge the death of his sister.

"I think we can work together. First I have to tell you that some of the things I do will be unconventional, highly illegal and that I'll be a wanted man by the police when this is over. Does that bother you?"

Wong looked out across the water and at the lights on the far side. His face worked, then he sighed. "I'm a banker, Mr. Hawke. A law-abiding man, something of a pillar in the Chinese community. I don't want to damage that positive influence if I can help it. But neither do I want to let the killers of my sister go unpunished. I can live with what happens here, as long as I don't have to do anything illegal. I owe that much to Shensi, to give those bastards a taste of what they must have done to her."

"Can I buy you dinner, Mr. Wong, and we'll talk some more?"

A half hour later they settled into a Chinese restaurant on

the fringes of Chinatown where many non-Chinese ate, and David Wong ordered for both of them. They were in the corner of the small, noisy room, and Matt was sure that no one could hear what they said.

"What I want you to do for me, Mr. Wong—"

"Please call me David."

"Fine. You call me Matt. Now, what I need you to do, David, is to get me to the right spots inside Chinatown, where I can find out what happened to Shensi. I need a handle, a starting point. Right now I have no leads at all. I would guess the police have about the same. It's my feeling that her death involved narcotics in some way, heroin."

"I know a lot of people in Chinatown," David said. "Some of them I have financed. Lots of them are in our Rotary club. But I can function without that much attention on me, right? I'll be in the background."

"I want you to stay out of danger. Your family has suffered enough. I'll never use your name and we'll keep you way back from the front lines."

"Good. That friend of mine I mentioned works with Group Forty-one of the DEA. He talks about it now and then. His group is concerned only with drugs in Chinatown."

"Interesting. You might be able to get some help for us from him—if he didn't know you were hunting it."

They finished dinner as they talked. While they sipped the final cup of green tea, Hawke leaned forward.

"Now for your first project. Where in Chinatown would be the best place to go to try to buy a large amount, say a pound, of uncut heroin?"

"You're talking a lot of money, I know that. I've heard of one place. It's the talk on the street, and my buddy Frank Edwards in the DEA has mentioned it too. It's the Golden Dragon. That's the most expensive nightclub and restaurant in Chinatown. Some nights it gets so full the fire marshal stops people from going in."

"Sounds like a good spot. Now, one more favor. I had a

friend in Vietnam who was proud that he came from Chinatown. He was a chopper pilot I got to know well. All I have is his name, Buzz Yuan. His real name was Walter.''

"First we check the telephone directory. Surprising how many people are in it with addresses and everything.'' David slid out of the booth and went to the telephones. He came back three minutes later shaking his head.

"No luck there. About how old is he?''

"Thirty-four, maybe thirty-five.''

David Wong snapped his fingers. His Oriental face broke into a big smile. "I almost forgot Mama Yuan. How could I not remember her? She's a nut about family and genealogy. She tries to prove that every Yuan is related to every other Yuan. If he's in any way related to her, she should know who he is. One more phone call.''

This time David stayed at the phone longer. He was talking and writing on a pad of paper. When he came back he grinned and held up the paper.

"Bingo! Your man is well known in some circles. Mrs. Yuan says she not only knows Walter Yuan but that he's her stockbroker. He lives in the Upper East Side Sixties—which is to say, he has more than a few bucks in his jeans—and he's unmarried, and she gave me his phone number.'' ·

Buzz. Hawke hadn't thought of the crafty young Chinese second lieutenant for years. He could make that chopper of his dart around like a hummingbird.

"I better try to call him. One man on my side in Chinatown will be good; two will be better.''

An hour later Matt Hawke walked in the Mandarin Garden on Pell Street and at once recognized Buzz Yuan where he stood talking with the hostess. Buzz looked up and grinned, then let out a whoop that caused a dozen people to turn and look at him. He ran to Matt and they shook hands, then hugged and clapped each other on the back.

"Ten years?'' Buzz asked. "I don't believe it. Ten years since 'Nam and those drinking sessions in Rosie's Bar.''

"More like thirteen or fourteen, but who the hell's counting. Stockbroker, huh? Big bucks. Thought you were going into the Peace Corps."

"I did too, but my father and my three uncles had other ideas. I'm Chinese—family means a lot. Especially a career. I really wanted to be a cop when I got back. Had my application in with the NYPD but I got talked out of it."

They went into the bar, ordered drinks, and kept talking.

"Remember the time we were out in the bush and you dropped me off right in the middle of a Cong ambush?" Matt asked, his eyes half closed and remembering. "First I caught all kinds of hell from a squad of North Viet' regulars. Then they threw a couple of hundred rounds at you and got lucky and hit your oil system, and your bird came down with a slow grinding set of rotors."

"Hey, no sweat on that one. I got away from my bird and stripped off my uniform shirt and had those jerks fooled for almost an hour thinking I was one of them."

"Sure you did, especially when you started shooting at them with that M-60 machine gun you always carried in your cockpit. How did you get hold of that anyway? I never did ask."

"On an evac, a kid brought it in and didn't make it back, so I just threw a blanket over it and appropriated it. My big trouble was getting boxes of link ammo!"

"If I hadn't shown up when the slants tried for you, with my six grenades and some M-16 persuasion, you'd be fertilizing some South Vietnam rice paddy about now."

"Damn straight!" They stared at each other.

"Christ! We made it out," Buzz snorted. "Sometimes I wonder how. Pure luck I guess. I know those were the days I thought I was gonna die young for sure. We both threw it around a little over there. You wound up with three silver stars didn't you?"

"Who's counting. That chopper of yours saved my butt more than once. Remember the time I was supposed to grab this headman and meet you at 1300 hours. You were there and no passengers."

"Glad I went hunting you. That chance patrol had you pinned down in that little wood lot between paddies."

"Yeah, I was dead meat that time. Booby traps all over the fucking place and I had this tied-up headman to lug along. How'en hell you ever fly the bird and use that M-16 out the door at the same time?"

"Skill, talent, brains, and a big batch of not giving a shit whether you die today or in thirty years."

"You really pulled my tail out of it that time."

They looked at each other and then started to laugh.

"We could tell war stories all night, Jarhead. Why are you in my big city? Last I knew you were headed for San Diego."

"I came up here to help a friend." Hawke took out the clippings about Shensi. There was a portrait when she was thirteen, the suicide notes from several girls, and a picture of the alley where they found Shensi's body.

"God! You knew her? I've been noticing these in the paper. Some cops think there's a pattern."

"I know there is. The pattern spells New Control."

Buzz's head snapped up. "Hey! That's a heavy name in this part of town."

"Ask Shensi, she knows exactly how heavy. Her brother said she was on the street. She ran away when she was thirteen. He found her when she was fourteen and she was doing tricks to support her horse habit. She ran away again. Next time he saw her was in the morgue. She must have hit the bottom hard. She got in trouble with New Control or they used her somehow, the way they used the other young Chinese dopers."

"You're guessing."

"Hell yes. That's all anybody can do. I need some help. My straight eyes and long nose don't fit in around here."

"You're talking wild side here, man!"

"Wilder the better. I remember somebody who used to say that."

"That was when I didn't care, and we were both in the fucking bush of 'Nam. Remember how cheap life was over there? One wrong step, put your head up at the wrong time, or just be in the wrong place at the deadly instant. None of us knew how long we were going to live, so we pushed it to the edge. It was wild side every time I took that bird upstairs. Here today, gone tomorrow...."

"But now you've got a Mercedes, a six-room apartment in the East Sixties, and you're pulling down a quarter of a million a year," Hawke said, looking at him evenly.

Buzz gave a sigh. "Close enough. More like half a mil this year." He sipped his drink, then looked up. "You got anything to work with? You aren't going in blind?"

"Almost. Nobody's got anything. I'm going in with a theory. Want to help me prove the theory?"

"We have tools of the trade that we had in 'Nam?"

"Best we can get. You know any underground arms dealers?"

"Oh shit! I can see one felony charge after another one. All I need is one felony conviction and I'm through in securities. No legitimate broker would even sniff at me." He shook his head and stared into his drink. "Hell, why not? I've been bored out of my skull lately. A little wild side will be fun for a change. Yeah, I know everybody. For an arms dealer it would take me a day or so. Might get some names tonight."

"You're on. Our first mission is nondestructive. A classical probe to test the enemy defenses."

"Like where?"

"The Golden Dragon."

"Oh, yeah, deep shit right off the bat. You know who runs that place?"

"Not the goofiest."

"Gent named Ali Sung. He tried to be Jewish, didn't

like it, so he became Muhammadan. He's an Islam Chinaman. The best intel says that he's buddy-buddy with the big boss who runs the New Control."

"Who runs it?"

"Nobody knows. From what I hear he's about thirty and from Hong Kong, maybe even a figurehead for one of the old Hong Kong triad outfits."

"Only one way to find out if we can connect."

"Yeah, but this mutha is a wild man."

"So we drop in and try him out. All we need to do is spread the word that we're looking to buy a pound of China White."

Buzz pretended to slip down in the booth. "A pound? Them slants over there give you mashed potatoes for brains on that last run across the wire? A pound . . . that's fifty, fifty-five thousand dollars!"

"Sixty. You ready to go? We might as well get this started."

"Right now?"

"Thought you liked to walk on the wild side, Buzz."

"That's why I never got married. Hell, let's give it a try."

Buzz watched Hawke. "Heard quite a bit of wild talk in the press about some gent named Matthew Hawke out in San Diego. Used to be in the DEA. Went crazy out there wiping out the drug operation in town and down in Tijuana. Could that have been you?"

"Coulda been."

"Then the same cat in Houston, same mission?"

"Different terrain, from Cal-Mex to Tex-Mex. Mandarin I don't *hablo*."

"Oh boy. Now Chinatown. You planning on using some heavy firepower?"

"Anything we can get our hands on from your contact."

"Yeah, I keep forgetting. This little girl?"

"She's the handle, the wedge. A way to get into the mob.

Just because they got slant eyes like you doesn't make them
any better than the Mexicans or the Mafia.''

"Yeah, true.''

"So how do we get to this Golden Dragon.''

"We take a cab.''

"My Mustang isn't good enough for you?''

They drove in the Mustang and parked around the corner
about a block from the Golden Dragon. Then they walked
inside. It was plush. It was expensive. They paid six dollars
each for drinks.

Hawke motioned the scantily clad Chinese cocktail waitress to bend closer.

"Sweetheart, I want to buy a pound of China White.
Who'en hell do I talk to? You point the way or send
somebody over.''

She shrugged and said something in Mandarin, then
walked away.

"She said she doesn't speak English,'' Buzz translated.
"She may be right. They bring in a lot of girls from Hong
King and Taiwan to work here.''

"You try it with the headwaiter,'' Hawke said.

When the headwaiter walked by, Buzz motioned to him
and talked in low tones in Chinese. The man shook his head
two or three times and at last walked away stiffly.

Hawke stepped out in front of him and they collided.
Hawke caught him so he wouldn't fall.

"Look, buster in a clown suit. I come in here to buy some
goods. I don't like getting the cold Chink shoulder, you
know what I mean? Now, you want me to make a scene? I
gotta start yelling my head off, or do we see somebody to
talk to?''

The headwaiter's eyes went wide; he backed away a step
and nodded. Then he scurried away.

They sat down and went back to their drinks. Five
minutes later a large Chinese man came to the table and
spoke softly to Buzz.

"Guy says we're to follow him," Buzz relayed.

They were twenty feet from the door when another man joined the group behind them and urged them toward the exit.

"Like in Rosie's Bar?" Buzz asked.

"On two," Hawke snapped. "Hut, two!" Hawke drove his elbow backward into the bouncer's stomach behind him, followed through with a spinning back fist and then a clean, short right cross to the point of the bouncer's chin. One foot sweep with his right foot knocked the last bit of stability from the tottering big man's body, and he crashed to the floor through a cocktail table.

Buzz took longer. He used a pair of lefts and rights to the Chinese bouncer's belly, then an uppercut to his chin and a lifted knee into the "security" man's crotch before he went down in a groaning pile on the floor.

When they walked back to their booth, their drinks were sitting where they had left them. They sat down and waited. No waiter or cocktail girl came near them. An hour later no one else had contacted them, so they paid the check, leaving no tip, and walked out.

The moment they touched the sidewalk below the canopy over the entrance, four huge Chinese men with two-foot-long red batons met them.

A fifth man stepped out of the shadows. "I understand you wish to talk with one of our salespeople. If you would be so kind as to follow me." He led the way up the sidewalk to the alley. Just inside the dark slot sat a brand new Rolls-Royce. The talker in the group held open the rear door and urged both of them to enter.

Sitting at the far side was a delicate Chinese girl with just enough makeup to enhance her natural beauty. The light remained on inside as the door closed.

"You're a hard lady to do business with," Hawke said gruffly. Then he smiled. "But your methods are effective. If we weren't serious, we would have left at the first invitation."

"You have a way of emphasizing your request with your physical ability," the girl said in a thoroughly American voice. "Were you serious about buying?"

"We are," Buzz said. "We have need now for a pound of China White, at least ninety-eight percent pure and uncut. We need it by noon tomorrow."

She watched both men. "What kind of references do you have? You both could be with the Forty-first Group."

"If we were DEA you'd be busted by now. We have the best references in the world, sixty thousand references, all in hundred-dollar bills," Hawke said.

She said something rapidly in Mandarin. Buzz made no attempt to translate, answering her instead in the same tongue. She shrugged.

"This is a trial run, to see if you can produce and to test the quality of your goods," Hawke said. "We know nothing of your reputation either. Do you have references?"

The girl laughed. Her voice sounded different, openly amused. "At least you have a sense of humor. It's nearly lacking in this business."

She watched them again. Slowly she lit a cigarette without inhaling and looked at the smoke. "You mentioned some code words inside, something about Rosie's Bar."

"Code words is right," Hawke said. "Rosie's Bar is the name of dozens of next-door native bars near half the bases in 'Nam when we both put in enough time. We worked together over there, too. No big mystery, just an action word."

"You have a territory in town?"

"Naw, not a chance. I'm from Jersey, up north. Won't touch your retail distribution operation here."

"If we agree on everything, and if your quality is as good as we've been led to believe," Buzz said, "we'll want up to twenty pounds a month."

"That's $1.2 million in cash a month up front," she said. "You two can handle that?"

"We can handle it, if you can supply it," Matt said. "Where and when?"

"Tomorrow morning at eleven, corner of Pell and Anvil. We'll make the delivery inside. Just the two of you."

"We'll be there."

She touched a control panel at her left hand and the door beside Hawke opened. They stepped out and walked back past the gaudily neon-lit club and caught a cab.

Hawke ordered the driver to go down a block and around the corner.

"Call me tomorrow," Hawke said. "I gave you my number. I'm going to see if I can tail that Rolls."

"Lots of Luck, jarhead," Buzz called.

The ex-Marine ran for his car, did a U-turn, and rolled back past the Golden Dragon. Down aways he saw the Rolls come out of the alley and turn ahead of him in the same direction. He pulled to the curb and waited for the big car to move half a block, then followed from well back.

It drove down Mott for three intersections, turned right for two, then stopped in front of a building half a block square that looked out of place, as if it had once been a midclass hotel. Hawke stopped half a block back and parked. He saw the same Chinese girl get out of the Rolls and walk up and into the big square building. He was sure that she used no key.

He watched the building for a while. No one came out. No one else went in. He drove past it. It was unnamed, unassuming. The building beside it had more class, and a better paint job.

A sign on the front of the smaller place modestly declared that the adjacent three-story establishment was the "Palace of Radiance and Beauty." It looked more like a women's gym.

An hour later Hawke was back at his hotel, with his car parked in the twelve-dollar-a-day garage—for hotel guests.

He called Buzz's home number and the ex-chopper pilot responded on the second ring.

"Buzz?"

"Jarhead?"

"So we go tomorrow. I've got the sixty from some leftovers. Real stuff. I'll meet you at Mott and Pell at ten-forty-five."

"Sounds good. You have sixty from leftovers?"

"Tell you about it later. I'd say three-piece suits will be in keeping with our lifestyle. Oh, any developments on our retail purchases of hardware?"

"Not much. Made one call and have a number. It was a no answer tonight. Tomorrow early. He's a friend of a friend who knows a place. I'll see if I can talk him out of the phone number."

"Catch you tomorrow."

Matt Hawke hung up and fell on the bed. He double locked the door and pushed a chair in front of it, then went to sleep before he had a thought of getting a shower.

At nine-thirty the next morning, Hawke met with Alfredo Marcello, a lawyer, member of the New York State Bar and the *consigliere* of the Bompensero Mafia family of New York. It had taken three phone calls to get through to the man, and a five-minute talk to persuade him to give Hawke a half hour of his time.

They met in a small Italian restaurant just above Canal Street in a part of Little Italy not far from Chinatown. The man was large, going to fat, with liver spots on his sallow face. He sipped the coffee and scowled.

"Damn right we hate the New Control. They cost us plenty. But the organizational structure of my business partners has moved in a different direction. We are businessmen. We have holdings in companies that might surprise you. One of my main jobs now is unfriendly takeovers of major corporations. We can make fifty, sixty million in a day with the stroke of a pen.

"That's why power and cash can do." He shook his head. "We have come a long way from the days you're thinking about, my young friend. We've graduated into bigger and far better things. Now we just leave the narcotics trade to the New Control and their Red Sticks."

"But you wouldn't mind giving them a black eye now and then. I heard that they cost you over twenty million last year alone in the Manhattan area."

"Fairy tales." He nibbled at a prune Danish, then looked up. "We hate the idea that they squeezed us out, sure, only natural. But we take a lot less flack from the politicians we own this way." He chuckled. "Why am I saying all this? I guess it's because I get the idea you're not exactly a law-abiding man yourself.

"You know some of the horse hitting the streets now is as high as forty-five percent pure? The junkies are blowing their heads off with that rich stuff." Marcello shrugged. "But, like I say, it really is out of our area of concern."

Hawke thanked him, picked up the check, then headed back to Mott Street and the meeting to buy sixty thousand dollars' worth of heroin.

It could be a start. Anyone selling this much, and up to twenty pounds a month, must be connected with the New Control. So far he had little to go on. This had to be a breakthrough. Finding Buzz was a stroke of luck. He grinned, remembering the way they had taken down the two Chinese bouncers last night in the club. It had been a case of total surprise, but anything that works.

He picked up Buzz on the corner of Pell and Mott as planned, drove down until he found Anvil, then parked a block away. When they got back to the street corner it was three minutes before the meeting time.

Two powerful looking young men wearing suits with red carnations in their lapels came up to them at once.

"You have an appointment at eleven?" one of the men asked.

Buzz replied in Chinese, Mandarin dialect, Hawke guessed. The four of them moved along half a block to a side street. You entered the first business on the street by going down steps. They took the steps, walked through a store that sold Chinese medicines, then into a hallway and on to a small room that was beautifully decorated with Chinese art and furniture.

The same small girl they met in the car sat behind a highly varnished black table. Directly behind her stood two Chinese men holding Ingram model 10 submachine guns. Both guns had forty-round magazines sticking out of the handle. The little weapons were less than eleven inches long.

She didn't rise. She looked at them and nodded. From under the table she took out a small package that was wrapped in a newspaper with Oriental characters.

"Good morning. You are prompt; we like that. My name is Lin Liu. I'll be your contact. Do you have the cash?"

Hawke took an envelope from the outside pocket of the suit jacket he wore. He moved slowly so the gunmen would not be alarmed.

Hawke walked up to the table and put down the white envelope beside the package. He waited while she looked at the bills. All were hundreds. She took them from the envelope and, quicker than a bank teller, she counted them.

She looked up amused and handed him back one of the hundred-dollar bills.

"There is no reason for a tip," she said. He took the bill with a grin and saw her lay the money down next to the package. He reached for the heroin, made a small cut in the newsprint near the top and wet his finger to pick up some of the powder. It was strong—pure heroin. He'd sampled horse before.

"Seems to be the right material. Did you bring a scale with you?"

She lifted out a finely balanced scale and handed it to him. He checked the one-pound weights, then put one of them on one of the small platforms and the heroin on the other. The heroin side was slightly heavier.

"The wrapping creates the differential," she said.

He nodded. Took the block of heroin, folded a copy of *The New York Times* around the drug, and stepped back.

"From what I've seen we should be able to do business on a regular basis. We'll be in touch with you about times and amounts. Do you give us a phone number or another address, or do we come to the Golden Dragon for a drink?"

"The Golden Dragon will be fine. I'm usually there when it's open. Ask the headwaiter to talk to me—never the waitresses."

Hawke nodded. He tried to read something into the girl's face, into her body language, into the way she spoke, but there was nothing there.

"Thanks, we'll be in touch."

He turned, and the men who had been behind them were gone. He and Buzz walked out of the small hallway and the shop with no problem. On the street they knew they were being watched. They stopped on the curb a moment.

"What the fuck are we going to do with a pound of uncut heroin?" Buzz asked.

"We're not selling it on the street, that's for damn sure," Hawke said. "We'll find a way to get rid of it. Down the toilet if no other."

They walked along the street. Half a block down they found a flower shop. Hawke pointed inside, and a few moments later he had bought thirty-three red carnations and had them delivered to Lin at the Golden Dragon as soon as it opened.

Buzz looked up at him in surprise.

"Thirty-three? How did you know about that? Three is a

lucky number for Chinese and thirty-three is nine times as lucky. Red is the New Control's color. Damn, you must know more about this operation than you've told me.''

Hawke laughed and paid for the flowers, and they walked back to his car. ''I'm no expert on you people, buddy. I just talked with the brother of the dead girl, David Wong. He's working with us on this. He helped me find you, remember?''

''Yeah, so what's next?''

''I'd really like to get a silenced Uzi chambered for 9-mm Parabellum, and some other toys. You have an address for us?''

CHAPTER
THREE

M ister Chu leaned against his stand-up desk facing a wall covered with pictures of beautiful women of all races in all stages of dress and undress. A glorious life-size nude by a good oil painter lounged across the center of the wall at eye level.

He was thirty-one years old, had been in New York for only four years after emigrating from Hong Kong, where he had been associated with one of the largest triads in that Crown Colony. Days there were numbered. He wanted a new power base, and he had contacted 14K with a suggestion. They had been interested.

Chu stood only five-feet-eight but wore lifts in his shoes to stretch him to five-ten. He had a stand-up desk to make him seem taller. He was slight yet trim, strong from growing up in the jungle of Hong Kong. Tough and gritty and more than a match for any man his weight. His face was marked on the cheek by a knife scar, and on his forehead was a jagged scar where he had been pistol-whipped in Hong Kong over a twenty-dollar whore. He lost.

He had come to New York through Canada, illegally one

bright spring day with a family of native New Yorkers. The immigration officer had asked the driver two questions and waved the car on through. Three of the "family" had been illegals.

Mister Chu wasn't looking at the pictures on his wall. For a moment he stared at a computer printout on his desk, then his gaze moved up and locked on a man standing beside him.

"Twenty-seven percent *decrease* in profit from your district, Han. Why?" Chu's face was calm, but the color rose in his neck and his hands trembled on the three-thousand-dollar walnut burl free-form top of his desk. Now he glared at the offending manager.

"I . . . I'm not sure, Mister Chu. I've been over all of the parameters, the input. The figures are accurate. Why the sudden decline in customers? . . . I just don't know."

"Find out, Han. Find out and correct it within the week, or you'll have a red stick in your hand again." Chu flared then, his face went red, and he lunged at the man. "Get him out of my sight!" he screamed. Han was quickly hustled out a door by a big Red Stick guard.

Mister Chu looked around. No one watched him. He settled back in front of his tall desk again and studied another report. He swept that and two or three more stacks of paper off his desk, turned to the window, and glared through it. The window faced the street. It was floor to ceiling and ten feet wide. He paced in front of it.

"Chen!" he demanded.

A short man wearing a suit and tie hurried up and stood near Chu.

"Are the shipments on schedule?"

"Yes sir. All three."

"What is our days' supply?"

"We currently have a fourteen DS, with normal sales. The next three shipments will be here within forty-eight hours."

"And what days' supply will that give us?"

"From a twenty-eight to a thirty-two DS, Mister Chu."

Chu nodded. Chen waited a moment, then backed away and returned to a bank of computers and printout machines across the forty-foot-long office.

Chu walked around the office and nerve center of his operation. From here he ran New Control. Drugs were only part of it. His men had developed a quickly effective protection racket with Chinese and other ethnic merchants in certain areas. That phase of the business was doubling each week.

The first meeting with a targeted merchant would bring an $888 "donation" to the Chinese Federated Charities. Then the merchant was instructed to have a thousand or two, or five thousand ready at the first of each month after that, depending on the size of the operation.

Loan-sharking was handled by other specialists. The lowest profit section was the girls. They were unreliable, they got sick, they got pregnant, they fought with each other, they died, they threw fits. But the prostitution end of the game was still Chu's favorite.

He paused now in front of Lin Liu. She stopped working on a keyboard and stood watching his face, waiting for him to speak.

"Why are we selling to a mixed white and red team?"

"For the profit," she answered quickly. "For the manpower involved, we can turn a profit of over three hundred percent in two hours as against what we could make on the street. On the street such a profit would take nearly two weeks, not counting all of the manifold risks and problems and personnel inadequacies that would be involved."

His anger faded. Slowly he nodded. "Yes, I agree. Continue the operation. It's for as much as twenty pounds a month?"

"Yes."

"Be sure to check with Chen for a continuing supply."

He moved on, and Lin Liu gave a relieved sigh and moved back to the computer terminal.

Mister Chu walked on past and watched the rest of his team of highly trained and intensely loyal workers as they functioned. There were fifteen in the room at the computers, the communications setups, and a radio net. Everything on the radio was in code. So far no one had broken it.

He watched the charts being turned out by computer showing sales for each territory last month, and in relation to a month ago and a year ago from each of the divisions: drugs, prostitution, gambling, and extortion.

Chu nodded. Moving nicely. All divisions. Only one or two of the tongs left in Chinatown were giving them any problems. Most of the tongs were now made up of ancient men who played mah-jongg for pennies every afternoon. He called them Old Chinwhiskers. They could help him little but they could hurt him. He would not allow it!

A tall, muscular young man with a red carnation in his lapel came in and stood six feet away, waiting for Chu to look at him. Mister Chu wondered how long this particular man would stand and wait. He had tested one of his people for a half hour one day. He waited without a word or a glance of unhappiness.

Now Chu looked at the man. "So?"

"We have him in our control, the one called Pigeon Heng. He's in the basement conference room."

"Bring him here. Now."

The Red Stick enforcer turned at once and hurried to the stairs. Five minutes later he came back with a wild-eyed young Chinese man with bruises on his face. One eye was closed and his nose still bled. His shirt had been half ripped off him. His arms were tied behind him by the wrists. As soon as he saw Mister Chu he fell on his knees, bent low until his head touched the floor.

He spoke rapidly in Mandarin, remaining in the position of respect. Heng knew he was fighting for his life.

"Yes, Mister Chu. I made a mistake. I'll never do it again. I was a retailer in Queens and I was behind on a debt, a gambling debt, and I used part of the receipts and didn't report them. Yes, I overcharged and recut, but I understand now. I'll be loyal. I'll never step one inch over the line again!"

"Enough!" Mister Chu shouted. "Stand up, I want to look you in the eye."

Heng stood, shaking so badly he had to keep moving his feet to keep his balance. Their stares met and Heng looked away quickly.

"You will not meet my eyes, traitor Heng? You say you will be loyal, but you show by your eyes that you will not. You are not worthy to be a member of the New Control."

Chu gave a hand signal and two men stepped forward and held the frightened man.

"Take him to the Camera Room," Chu said.

Pigeon Heng screamed all the way to the stairs, then one of the Red Sticks hit him in the mouth with the heavy red baton, smashing three teeth, and he choked off his screams as he sobbed.

When Mister Chu walked into the Camera Room ten minutes later, everything was ready. The room was brightly lighted. A three-quarter-inch Betacam video camera sat on a tripod. The cameraman was well back but had the zoom lens focused up close.

A large Red Stick guard stood ready on each side of Heng. He was blubbering, twisting trying to get away. The red baton slammed into his kidney and he screeched and sagged to that side. The Red Stick guards held him upright.

Mister Chu put on a protective plastic gown and watched Heng.

He walked into the camera's range and looked back at the operator. The man nodded.

"Action," the cameraman said.

Mister Chu moved forward and lifted Heng's chin with

his hand. "Pigeon Heng, you have violated your oath, you have stolen from the New Control, you have violated every trust placed in you. There is only one way you can repay us."

Heng screamed at the camera. "No, no!" he bellowed.

In the viewfinder of the video camera, the face of Mister Chu never showed. He could not be identified. Now the lens pulled back to show more of the scene. The Red Sticks pushed Heng down to the floor in a kneeling position. A two-foot-square butcher's block stood there, and they pressed Heng's head down on the block. His left ear was smashed hard against the laminated wood. The stout Red Sticks' red batons pushed down hard from each side and held Heng's head firmly on the block.

Heng's screams filled the small room.

Mister Chu ignored them, took a tool from a third Red Stick guard, and lifted it over his head.

Mister Chu gave a grunt and then a cry of vengeance as he brought the heavy Chinese war ax down with all his power.

The two-foot-long ceremonial ax, with a swept-up eight-inch-wide blade, drove straight down, touched Pigeon Heng's neck, and chopped through it into the sturdy block.

The men released the red batons and Heng's head quivered on the block for a moment from the force of the blow, then slowly rolled off the block to the plastic-sheeted floor. The head bounced and then turned until the vacant, open eyes seemed to stare directly into the camera lens as the operator pushed the focus lever on the zoom to bring the face up to fill the screen. Only a small amount of blood drained from the neck as gravity took over from the heart's pressure.

There was total silence in the room.

Two of the red batons came down, crossing in front of the face.

"Cut," Mister Chu said. He carefully took off the plastic gown and dropped it on the headless body.

Without a word he left the room and walked back up one flight to his apartment. Each recruit to the New Control would have the opportunity to see the most recent disciplinary action. Loyalty to the New Control would be maintained at any cost.

The other half of the ancient execution blood ritual still had to be completed. He walked into his apartment, a lavishly decorated and furnished six rooms on the top floor. Two girls in the living room stood quickly when he came in.

Both were topless and wore the smallest bikini swimsuit briefs they could find.

He smiled at them and waved for them to follow him. They went through two rooms into his bedroom. Already Mister Chu had slid out of his three-thousand-dollar pure silk suit coat and tore at the buttons on his shirt. Both girls helped him.

An hour later Mister Chu had dressed and returned to the office section of the top floor. He leaned on his stand-up desk and looked out over New York. Out of the corner of his eye he saw Harry Han come up and stand waiting in the appointed place.

Harry was an important cog in the machinery. Mister Chu turned at once and nodded. Harry came closer. He had a worried expression. Mister Chu waited.

"Harry?"

"Nothing earthshaking. Understand they found Heng. I was just wondering—we could use people like him in our throne chair."

Mister Chu snorted. "They wouldn't cooperate, would they?"

"Wouldn't matter. We tie them in place and a volunteer gambler pays an extra thousand to spin the cylinder and pull the trigger. Hell, I'd even do it myself."

"You'd enjoy that, wouldn't you, Harry."

The other man nodded. "Always have. I just saw Mr. Heng's final seconds. Interesting."

"You get your rocks off watching it?"

"Yeah." He was not defensive, simply agreed.

Mister Chu laughed. "You are one of a kind, Harry. A true unique personality. All right. The next time we have the need to eliminate one of our own, or someone else, we'll confer about the practicality of the game. You have a candidate for the chair this week?"

"Not yet, but we'll keep watching. Not much of a shortage, really just a matter of selection and preparation."

"You need a new writer for your suicide notes, Harry. You see the newspaper?"

"Yeah, we talked about it. There will be no more dictating by Willy. We'll start earlier and let them write on and on if they want to. He's been disciplined."

"How about a black or an Italian next time? Mix up the cops a little."

Harry nodded. Mister Chu turned and the interview was over. He snapped his fingers and a trio of girls stepped up. They were dressed alike, all in red miniskirts and red blouses. Their hair was long and straight with bangs in front. They were alike in other ways, too, with good figures, pretty faces, and wide smiles.

"Bring the car around," Mister Chu said. "I want a tour of some of the problem areas."

The three girls carried large purses. In each purse was an unsilenced Ingram M-10 submachine gun that could spit out .45 slugs at the cyclic rate of 1,145 rounds per minute. The girls were known as the three princesses, and Mister Chu never traveled without them. They were his favorite bodyguards and doubled as extermination experts as they were needed.

The girls cleared the way to the private elevator, and one went down first and sent the lift back up, covering the first floor with her hand inside her purse.

When the elevator came down and stopped, the first girl hurried outside and moved ten yards up the street in front of the stretch limousine that had pulled in at the curb. The second princess came out and stood guard in the other direction.

The third girl walked beside Mister Chu as they went quickly to the limo and got into it. The two remaining girls got in one car in front and one behind the head man, and the three-car caravan moved out into the afternoon traffic.

The first stop was a small Chinese acupuncture office on Mott Street. Two Red Stick men walked inside first, then the two girls from the front and back cars. When all was ready, Mister Chu and the other princess with her submachine gun walked into the building.

It was set up much like any medical office: a half dozen chairs in a reception room, a door, and a window where a woman looked out. She wore medical whites.

A small bald man with thick glasses hurried through the connecting door into the waiting room.

"So this is the famous Mister Chu," he said with a sour tone. His face was angry, his hands busy. "I am not amused. Kindly leave my property. I have work to do."

He started to turn when one of the princesses did a quick spinning back kick and slammed her heel deeply into the small man's chest just below his rib cage. He went down on the floor bellowing in pain.

One of the Red Sticks lifted him up.

"You will go now and bring back three hundred thirty-three dollars initiation costs," the Red Stick guard said. "You will pay our representative a thousand dollars a month or your establishment will be demolished, and your life will hang on the good will of Mister Chu." He held out his hand.

The small acupuncturist stumbled into the back room and came out a few minutes later with a stack of money. The guard counted out the stipulated amount and gave the rest back.

"Dr. Sun," Mister Chu said, speaking for the first time.

"If you'll be reasonable, then we'll be reasonable." He flicked his hand and the first two princesses left to guard the street. When it was secure he walked out and into the armor-plated stretch Lincoln limousine, and it drove away shepherded by the other two cars.

They made four more stops and at last pulled into a narrow street in the northern part of Queens, just off Grand Central Parkway. It was a characterless house, in the old style, three stories, built solid and square.

The girls were less watchful here but did their job. Inside, a small Chinese woman hurried up and chattered with Mister Chu in Chinese, then nodded and bowed. She left and came back quickly with a young man who was ill at ease but not at all frightened. Two Red Stick guards had been on hand when the three cars arrived.

Mister Chu smiled at the young man and motioned him over to a window that looked out into a garden. It was still afternoon, and ten or twelve women in various degrees of undress sat in the sun or lay on lounges. Three wore nothing at all.

Mister Chu watched the girls and smiled, then talked to the young man a few moments. From his pocket he took a wad of bills held together with a golden clip. He took off five one-hundred-dollar bills and pressed them into the young man's hand.

They both nodded and the contingent left. It wasn't until they were outside that the young man looked at the bills. He smiled, slapped the small woman playfully on the side of the head, and ran out into the courtyard screeching and laughing.

David Wong finished his duties at the bank. As a loan officer he had no more appointments and at five he left promptly and hurried home. Jasmine said she would be there tonight and they could have dinner before she went to the show. He lived in an apartment in the northern edges of Chinatown not far from Little Italy.

As soon as he came in the door he knew Jasmine was there. She was cooking dinner, a cross between a traditional Chinese type and what smelled like sauerkraut and wieners.

He often wished she would get married, but his own example of bachelorhood was not much incentive to her. She usually lived with two other dancers farther uptown.

Jasmine grinned at him as soon as she saw him. "Hi, bruthua," she said, giving it a black pronunciation.

"Yeah, mama!" he growled and they both laughed. They had been close after their parents died. Now they were drifting apart.

"How is the show going?"

"Great!" she said. "I just wish more of the dancers would get sick or pregnant or something. Maybe one of them could break her leg!"

He frowned.

"Not really. They are all such great girls. But as swing dancer I just get to dance when one of them is off. Which is not every night. But they still pay me. On my next show I'm going to get a full-time performing slot."

Jasmine looked like a dancer. She was five-three, slender, with high tight buns and legs that could kick the ceiling. She'd started with classical ballet training, then jazz and modern, and finally studied with a woman who taught nothing but Broadway show dancing.

Her hair was shoulder length but usually hidden under a wig to fit the part. Now she wore a sweatshirt with holes in it that was half again too big for her. She had on whitewashed blue jeans and Nike sneakers.

"It is sauerkraut," David said, lifting a pot lid on the gas burner.

"Right, hot dogs and kraut and eggrolls with sweet and sour sauce. What could be more Chinese?"

They had a good talk during dinner and both cried when

they spoke about Shensi. Jasmine had to go then and ran to catch the subway to take her up to Times Square and the Forth-eighth Street theater.

David Wong made some more phone calls. He figured the more he could find out about the New Control the better. He learned little and caught a suspicious note from one man. He quickly said he was interested because of a bank loan reference and hung up.

He sat at the kitchen table and dialed the phone. The hotel rang Hawke's room but there was no answer. If there were anything else Hawke wanted him to do, he would give a call.

Just after Hawke sent the red carnations to Lin Liu at the Golden Dragon, Buzz said he had nailed down the phone number of a gent who might be able to help them with some weapons.

"Now, we didn't spell out anything on the phone, and he said I'd have to call back today and he'd look us over. To be in the kind of area he's probably in, we shouldn't be wearing these duds or packing sixty thou in uncut China White."

"Come to my place and we'll change."

"First we stop on Canal Street at one of those surplus places, and we both can pick up some spare fatigues and undercover clothes. They'll fit in better in the neighborhood where I bet we're headed."

They found what they wanted on Canal Street. It was a half mile of the great American flea circus and swap meet all rolled into one. They each got a pair of chino pants, fatigues, and some shirts as well and drove to Hawke's hotel.

Hawke stashed the heroin under the mattress and they changed, then, looking more suited to the rabble, they went back to the street and Buzz made his phone call.

A half hour later they found the place over in Brooklyn. It

was on the edges of a business–light industrial area that had gone from bad luck to worse. The man wouldn't commit himself to anything until he saw them.

The address was a small hardware store with iron bars still on the front windows and the front door. But it was unlocked. They walked inside and saw that it was an old-fashioned hardware, with nuts and bolts, nails in bins, a claw and sacks, and even butt hinges in little cardboard boxes, not in plastic sacks.

A black man with a full beard watched them as they walked in. There was nobody else there.

"Yeah, watjawant?"

"Buddy?" Buzz asked.

"True. Who's askin?"

"Buzz—I called you while ago."

"Yeah. Who's the other dude?"

"I'm Hawke."

"Damn good name. Good idea. The hawks get. The pigeons pay."

"Need some goods, Buddy. Hope this wasn't a wild-goose chase out here."

"Depends."

"We don't dicker much on price," Hawke said.

Buddy looked at them.

"How I know you ain't some of them tobacco and firearms guys?—shut me up tight and throw me in the slammer."

"Gotta trust somebody, Buddy," Hawke said. "Some jaspers over in Chinatown messed with this little girl, hooked her on horse, and got her on her back, then blew her brains out. She was fifteen, Buddy. Seen it all, done it all, and paid the price. We aim to even up the score a little."

"Lordy, lordy. I stay off that shit. Had me a boy who took the whole nine yards; he paid, too. Dead and gone near a year." Buddy brushed moisture from his rough black cheeks and motioned to them.

"Let me lock the front door and we'll go downstairs to the playground." He came toward them and reached up. "Mind if I check you for wires? Feds get damn tricky sometimes."

He patted them down, on chest, back, and legs where a small transmitter might be taped, nodded, and locked the door.

The basement was a small ordnance room.

"I was an armorer with the Fortieth Division back in Korea," Buddy said. "Really like guns. Put them together, repair them, all that shit. Then I started getting some that the law said I shouldn't. Moved it all down here and been having fun ever since. Now and then I get a call for some goods."

Hawke looked around. The place was a gunsmith's dream. Metal lathes to make parts, assembly tables, loading equipment for filling shells with powder and lead.

One whole wall was covered with weapons hung on pegboard. There was everything from a derringer to a .44 Automag.

"This stuff for sale?" Hawke asked.

"I'll sell anything but my wife," Buddy said. "That's only cause I tried and I couldn't even give her away!" He roared at his own joke.

Hawke found a little-used .45 autoloader, and Buzz took a Beretta 93-R, a snazzy little self-loading pistol that would fire single shot or in three-round bursts of 9-mm Parabellum.

"Fraggers and C-3 or C-4?" Matt asked.

Buddy shrugged. "You guys are going in hard I'd say. Hell, I aim to please." He lifted a wooden box filled with old style fraggers, the hand-size type with the deep grooves in the casing.

Hawke picked out half a dozen and then checked over a smaller box with quarter-pound squares of C-3 plastic explosive.

"This stuff still stable?" Hawke asked.

"Hey, if it wasn't, would I be storing it down here under my shop and my house?" Buddy asked.

Hawke took six of the chunks and six detonator-timer combinations. He got two boxes of .45 rounds and five for the Beretta in 9-mm Parabellum.

"Ingrams or Uzis?" Buzz asked.

Buddy shook his head. "Figure if you can't hit it with a three-round burst, you best leave it in your bunker."

"True."

He watched them. "You boys in 'Nam?"

"Right," Buzz said. "We both did our time there. Fired a shot or two in anger."

He didn't push it.

Hawke saw an M-16 with an M-203 grenade launcher attached below the barrel, but he passed on it. Their work was going to be up close and dirty. An Ingram would have been handy.

Buddy pulled up a weapon from behind a bench.

"You get serious about making bodies dead, nothing can beat this one." He laid a Spas-12 on the table in front of them. It was a semiautomatic shotgun. It was only a little over twenty-eight inches long and would hold nine rounds of double-aught buck in a twelve-gauge size. It was gas operated. Pull the trigger and every time it goes bang.

"Yeah!" Buzz said, looking at it. He grabbed it, picked it up with one hand, then quickly brought the other up to the front grip. "Daddy, buy me this!" he crooned.

"Crowd control!" Hawke said and smiled.

Fifteen minutes later they had looked over the rest of the merchandise and decided they had enough. The bearded man totaled the purchases on a small calculator.

"Five thousand seven hundred eighty," he said.

"What?" Buzz bellowed.

"Sold," Hawke said. "Buzz, we're spending their money against them. I don't mind it when an honest merchant makes a profit."

Buzz shook his head. "Buddy, how long does it take you to take in that much cash upstairs?"

Buddy chuckled. "A year, year and a half."

"Thought so."

Hawke took a roll of bills out of his pocket and began counting out piles of ten one-hundred-dollar notes. He made it six stacks even.

"The two hundred twenty is a tip," Hawke said.

They put the merchandise in two cardboard boxes and carried them out to the rented Mustang's trunk.

"You think we should be packing now?" Buzz asked.

"No. We could get busted if a cop stopped us for a parking ticket. Let's wait until we need to carry the weapons."

"How about needing them today?" Buzz asked. "The market's closed and I've shot a whole day."

"Maybe we can. We should spend the rest of the afternoon on a look-see job. Then I'll call David Wong tonight. He might have something for us."

"Lead on, Sarge. I'm putting my butt on the line for you again, but what the hell. Who wants to live forever?"

CHAPTER
FOUR

Hawke knew they should be dirtier, but they sprawled and crumpled on the sidewalk across from the building where Lin Liu had vanished the night before. Both had paper sacks holding a drink, which were supposed to look like wine, which would make them winos, real bums on the town for an afternoon of sun before the colder night dropped into Manhattan.

Actually, the sacks held cans of Coke, and the caffeine was about all that was keeping them awake. The sun was warm, no one stepped on them, and they were out of the foot traffic.

"Man, bums really have it terrible!" Buzz wheezed softly as he changed positions on the concrete. "This stuff is harder than hell!"

Hawke agreed with him. They saw what could have been the same Rolls they had sat in the night before pull up, and three people got out. They went up the steps and into the square-cut six-story building and through the front door without the aid of keys, knocks, or a guard. The Rolls moved down the street and out of sight.

All the people in the group had been Chinese, well dressed but not flashy. None of them wore a red carnation.

"So what the hell we looking for?" Buzz asked.

"Some of your rich customers down here slumming. You have mostly Chinese customers or others?"

"Others. I work almost exclusively with big corporate accounts and large retirement funds. That way I don't have to do much advising, just buy and sell."

"What's the place next door, that Palace of Radiance and Beauty?" Hawke asked.

"Damned if I know. Maybe a beauty college or a repair joint for women." He laughed. "Last date I had, now there was a dame who could use some radiance and beauty."

A well dressed Chinese woman came down the street carrying a cardboard box. She stopped at a man sitting on the curb and gave him something. Then she headed for Hawke and Buzz. She stared at Buzz a minute, then without a word handed him a small paper sack. She went to Hawke and peered at him.

"Down on your luck, young man?" she asked.

Hawke nodded. She gave him a sack. "Things will be better, soon. Don't give up hope," she said and moved on.

Hawke looked in the sack. It held a homemade sandwich wrapped in waxed paper and an apple.

Buzz was already munching into his food.

"Thought they said there wasn't any free lunch," Buzz said.

Hawke watched the woman. He stood and caught up with her. She looked at him.

"Still hungry?" she asked.

"No. You do this all the time? Give away food this way?"

"Most days, on my lunch break. I know—my friends say what's the use. But it makes some people happy, feeds them something other than wine, and it just might help. Doesn't cost much."

Hawke pulled two bills off the roll in his pocket and pressed the two hundred dollars into the woman's hand.

"Keep up the good work," he said and walked quickly up the street toward Buzz. Hawke didn't see the delighted smile that broke over the woman's face as she looked at the bills. "Let's get out of here, we're wasting our time," Hawke said and kept moving. Buzz followed, scratching his chest.

They went back to Hawke's hotel room. Hawke tried to call Wong but he had left work and wasn't home yet. They went out for dinner and when they came back, they called again. Wong was home and excited.

"I've got something that will interest you," Wong said.

"Good, we'll meet you at your place. You said you have a buddy on Group Forty-one of the DEA."

"Yes."

"Good. Tell us how to get to your place; we'll come right over."

A half hour later David Wong looked at the package wrapped in a Chinese newspaper Buzz said was from Hong Kong.

"What is it?" David asked.

"Take a look," Buzz said.

He opened it and saw the white powder.

"It isn't really," Wong said, stepping back.

"Won't hurt you," Hawke said. "I want you to give this to your contact at Group Forty-one. Tell him a friend bought it after a meet at the Golden Dragon. They work out of a Rolls-Royce."

"He'll ask me a lot of questions." Wong shook his head. "No, bad move. I'd rather just melt it and flush it down the toilet. How can I explain to him where I got sixty thousand dollars' worth of heroin?"

"Your call," Hawke said. "What's your news?"

"My friend in Group Forty-one told me about a place he is sure is a cutting room for heroin. But every time they get there it's clean as a operating room. They use a search warrant and that evidently tips off the dopers."

"I never use a search warrant. You have an address?"

"I can get it."

"Tell him your new friend wants to observe the place. Can't hurt."

A little over an hour later, Buzz and Hawke watched a small, middle-class house from across the street. They had parked a block down and walked here in the darkness.

"Buzz, I know it's been a long time since 'Nam. We were wasting the Cong there for legitimate and legal reasons. We had no problem with that. Now it's a different war. Do you really want to go this far on the wild side? This one night could ruin your life, slam-dunk you into a prison cell. I was wondering, can you pull the trigger when you look at some Chinese faces?"

"Hell, yes! to all of that. These are slimeballs twenty times as bad as any slope I ever wasted in 'Nam. Hell, yes, I can pull the trigger. Just because we both have slanted eyes makes no difference. I know what that shit does to people, and I'm as furious at them as you are. I just never had a chance to show them before. Don't worry about me, old leatherneck. I'll be slinging lead when the time comes."

"Had to check," Hawke said. "It's routine for me now. These are animals that need to be obliterated, smashed, pulverized. But I owed it to you to ask before you got in over your head."

"One request," Buzz said, looking up. "Just make fucking sure that we get away from here. I don't want to get pulled in on a felony charge."

"No sweat, chopper topper. Let's go."

This was a middle-class neighborhood in Queens near Jackson Heights. Two cars were in the driveway. Lights had come on upstairs, and they saw that there were lights in the half-basement windows.

Matt had the Spas-12 combat shotgun loaded with double-aught buck, and the .45. Buzz carried the squirt gun Beretta 93-R, a pair of hand grenades, and two blocks of the C-3 and detonators.

They watched the place for a half hour and nobody went in or out. They split and came at the house from opposite directions. Hawke carried the shotgun tight to his chest so it couldn't be spotted. They slid into the yard on either side of the house and ran to the back. Blinds covered the windows. A rear door led down to the half basement.

Hawke tried the knob on the door at the bottom of the steps. Locked. It opened inward. Hawke used a set of picks on the door, then gave up and slid the small blade of his knife against the locking bolt and bit by bit wedged it back into the door. A moment later the panel came free and pushed inward an inch.

They listened. Nothing. They edged the door open farther and saw a second door six feet ahead. This part of the basement seemed to be used as a storage area. Light came from under the bottom of the second door. Now they could hear voices beyond.

"You got the left half, I've got the right," Hawke whispered. "Once we use the weapons we won't have much time. Neighbors will be all over the place."

They each took one of the blocks of C-3 plastic explosive and pushed the detonator into the soft material.

"Set them for thirty seconds," Hawke said. "That will be time enough. Then all we do is lay them down, push the activating lever, and we're out the back door if it's still clear."

Buzz nodded and they stepped up to the door. It opened inward. Buzz tried the knob. It was not locked. He eased the door in an inch, looked at Hawke.

"Now," he said softly. They jolted the door inward and they charged through the door shoulder to shoulder.

In flash recognition, Hawke saw the cutting table, the six

hard cases doing the mixing, measuring and weighting the goods.

"They're all dirty!" Hawke bellowed and triggered the first blast from the Spas-12. The double-aught buck caught the first two hardcase Chinese in the midsection. They worked at the near end mixing and measuring the heroin.

The buck drove them back six feet, nearly cut them in half, and dumped them into eternity in the blink of a cosmic second.

Buzz saw three men on his side of the long table. He squirted three rounds of 9-mm Parabellum hot lead down the row, which took out two of the men. One of the rounds hit the middle man in the chest, smashing through a rib and churning the left ventricle of his heart, killing him instantly. The last man on the table had just lifted a box of paper packets of heroin. The rising round caught him under the chin and slammed through his mouth into his brain.

The third one closest got special, individual treatment. Buzz fired again and three Parabellum rounds drilled neat holes from his chin to his forehead, slamming him over the table and leaving him dead where he fell.

Hawke used another round of double-aught buck. The last man at the far end of the table drew an automatic and had it up almost ready to fire when the expanding pattern of double aught spattered across his chest, pulping his flesh, smashing half his ribs and ripping ten holes in his lungs. He went down with a froth of blood on his lips before he knew it, and blood poured out his nose as he tried to breathe.

Hawke and Buzz looked at each other. Each put a quarter-pound block of plastic explosive on the cutting table, pushed the activating lever, and then both men ran for the rear door.

They were out of the basement and into the darkness of the backyard before they heard the neighbors. Somebody called from next door.

Hawke and Buzz went over a six-foot chain link fence

behind the house, dropped into a backyard, and sprinted for the street past the closest side of the house. They made the street and were half a block down when the C-3 triggered. The explosions shattered windows for six houses around, tore the frame two-story house into kindling, and started a fire. The fire turned into a roaring blaze fed by the open three-quarter-inch high-pressure gas line that had erupted in back of the regulator.

It was a fire that would not be put out until the gas was shut off at the street. By the time they moved down the sidewalk and back within a block of the fire where they had left the rented Mustang, there were a hundred people watching the blaze. Nobody tried to put it out because it had come too fast and was too big.

Buzz and Hawke stepped into the Mustang just as a police car whined around the corner, its red lights blinking. They let it pass, then eased away from the curb and drove out of the area before the first fire unit responded.

"How much shit do you think was on the table?" Buzz asked as they stopped a mile down the street and stowed the weapons and ordnance back in the closed cardboard boxes in the Mustang's trunk.

"Maybe twenty pounds," Hawke said. "They wouldn't get a crew together to work less than that."

"Twenty pounds is $1.2 million worth," Buzz said. He whistled. "Yeah, now that is a jolt that even the New Control bunch will feel. Street value should have been at around three times that, or $3.6 million smackerooners! Now we are starting to talk serious money."

"Which means the New Control is going to make a serious effort to find out who trashed their cutting operation. They know Group 41 of the DEA doesn't work that way. A rival gang? It would grab the goods, not destroy them. New Control is gonna be damned upset."

A short time later they hit traffic getting over the Triborough Bridge.

Buzz was still riding a wave of the emotion that charged through him well after the attack on the cutting house.

"Christ! Just like in 'Nam when my bird went down and we had to plow through about a thousand Cong to get back to that advanced base camp, remember? I'm still pumped! It went so fucking fast! Bam! Brrrrrrrt. Bam! Blast, blast, and it's over. We drop the C-3 and split out and over the fence."

He turned off the radio and looked at Hawke. "We couldn't have been in that basement more than twelve or thirteen seconds! We were fast and we were good. Jesus, but I love that Beretta 93-R. What a sweetheart."

By the time they got back to Manhattan, Buzz had mellowed out a little.

"Hey, I got to work tomorrow. Don't plan any fun and games without me. I'll give you a call tomorrow night and see what's cooking. You need help, count on me. I even know where I can get a chopper. A rental place right here on Manhattan, over on the Hudson way down by the Battery."

Hawke dropped Buzz at his uptown condo apartment building and drove back toward his hotel down near Fourteenth Street. It had been a good day's work, but it was only a start. Who ran the New Control? Where was their headquarters? How could he use Lin Liu to get a line on them?

It was early when he parked and went up to his room. There had been one message. A note from David Wong that said he had two tickets for Jasmine's show the next night at eight-thirty and that Hawke should be there and bring along a friend.

Hawke watched TV for a while and went to bed. He needed a good night's sleep for a change.

The next morning he spent his time trying to locate one of the tongs, the Chinese societies that used to run Chinatown. He stopped by at David's bank and David gave Hawke three names. When Hawke tried to talk to the men involved, he found none of them in their places of business.

The *Times* had a short front page story on the heroin

cutting laboratory that exploded and burned the previous evening. The story left a lot unsaid.

"Six unidentified persons died in a residence in Jackson Heights last night when it blew up and burned to the ground. Neighbors reported two heavy explosions that shattered windows in surrounding houses. Police and fire officials were saying little about the situation, but the presence of narcotics task force NYPD officers meant that narcotics were involved in the affair.

"One NYPD spokesman said off the record that the house had been used in the past as a cutting house. It was where heroin was 'cut,' or diluted by being mixed with filler material, before it was sold on the streets. The same source said the house had been under suspicion for some time. Ambulance personnel at the scene reported that six bodies were removed from the basement and that all had been burned beyond identification.

"The police and narcotics investigation is continuing."

As soon as the Golden Dragon opened at two, Hawke went in and asked the headwaiter if he could see Lin Liu. Five minutes later as he waited at the bar, he was told she was not in. He couldn't get any other information about her.

Hawke called Buzz at work and found that he had left. He called his home and caught him. Hawke had left a message earlier about the show tickets to see *Stomping in Manhattan*. They agreed to meet at the box office at eight that evening.

Hawke walked around Chinatown but had no idea how to nail down exactly who and where the New Control was. He had to work through his sources.

Later he went to his hotel and called David Wong at work. Wong said he had nothing new. He had decided to flush the heroin down the toilet but he wanted Hawke as a witness. He would do it as soon as Hawke came over.

"Could you come right after work, in about an hour?" Wong asked. "I hate to have that stuff around my place."

Hawke went to the apartment, and they cut up the block

of pure heroin and let it melt in the sink and the toilet bowl, then washed it away.

Wong wiped sweat from his forehead. "Damn glad to have that stuff gone. Now go and enjoy the show. Oh, I told Jasmine you'd be coming. Be sure to go backstage afterward and see her. She always likes to have people come back."

The show was a midseason revue type and held up well because of the great songs and good dancers. There was only one Chinese girl in the chorus line, and they assumed she was Jasmine.

After the show they went back and met her. She was as charming as her big brother, and much prettier. She was polite to Hawke but when she looked at Buzz, even Hawke could see the sparks. Buzz reacted in nearly the same way.

"Look, would both of you like to come out for a snack? I never eat before a show, and I'm supposed to eat something so I don't get anorexic." She asked the question of them both, but she was looking only at Buzz.

"I'd like to, but I just can't," Hawke said. "Early day tomorrow. Fact is, I better split right now. It was a great show, Jasmine, and you did very well. I hope it runs for years."

She kissed his cheek. "Thank you, nice man. My brother was right about you."

They said good-bye and Hawke went out to find his car. There was a parking ticket on it. He threw it in the back seat and drove down to his hotel. On an impulse he kept on driving to the Golden Dragon and parked down the street.

Inside, as he came in, the headwaiter stared at him and motioned.

"Miss Liu is here now. May I take you to her table?"

Hawke nodded. A strange ripple went down his back and he smiled. She was a beautiful girl, and she was his one contact that had to be with the New Control.

She sat with her back to him, but he knew it was she the moment he saw her. Her long black hair was swept up on top of her head with the ends cascading down. Her dress was all black, formfitting, and strikingly beautiful.

He stood in front of her table for a moment, and when she looked up her face showed the hint of a smile.

"Please sit down, Mr. Twenty Pounds. That's the only name I have for you."

He grinned and sat. Tonight she had dressed for the evening, not as a businesswoman, and the effect was stunning.

"Is this always your office? Do you rent this table by the week?"

A waitress set a drink in front of him and another one of the same kind in front of Lin.

"My compliments, Mr. Twenty," she said. They both sipped their drinks. "I've checked with my people and we can handle your order on a continuing basis. I hope that's good news."

Hawke nodded. He had no idea what the drink was. He decided to go easy on it.

"In a way, it is good news. Now I can contact my finance people and tell them to send me the first $1.2 million."

"To a lasting relationship," she said.

"Here here." He sipped the drink. Strange.

"So is this your office?"

"Of course not. A lot of business is done over drinks and dinner. Both here are tremendously average. But it's close, it has a good name, and most people can find it."

Hawke thought she seemed nervous, ill at ease. She looked around the club. Now she was relieved. Her glance came back to him. "I'm sorry, I was expecting someone."

"Another twenty?"

"Not even a ten," she said. "But a customer is a customer."

"Are you asking me to leave?" he said.

"Oh no!"

"Good. It's only slightly after midnight. Closing time is a long way off."

"Your office is in New Jersey, you said."

"That's right—quite a drive from here."

She saw someone or had a signal. "I'm sorry, but it looks like I'm the one who is going to have to leave. I'll go to the ladies' room. Please don't leave for five minutes, and then it'll be all right. I'm fine; don't concern yourself."

She stood, he got up, and she left. Hawke sat down again and tasted the drink. Not something he wanted to finish, he was sure. He toyed with it for a couple more minutes, then slid over and got out of the booth. What a crazy contact that had been.

When he walked out he noticed nothing unusual. No one followed him. In situations like this he felt as if he were hitting the bush in 'Nam with the slopes all around him. He always watched his tail.

Hawke breathed a short sigh of relief when he walked to the curb, and another when he saw his car parked where he had left it. Car thieves were murder in the city, any city. He unlocked the driver's side and started to slide in. He brought his head down and looked inside.

Lin Liu sat in the passenger's seat.

"I would appreciate it if you could drive away from this area right away, Mr. Twenty," she said, sending him a smile that was tinged with a periphery of fear.

CHAPTER
FIVE

Hawke drove away from the Golden Dragon with Lin Liu beside him. He looked over at her once, but her expression had not changed. It was one of grim, almost fatalistic determination edged with a deep, numbing fear.

"Are you running away from them?"

"No."

"Call me Matt."

They were silent as he drove toward the Hudson River. He stopped near the chopper pads and parked so they could look out across the water at the New Jersey lights on the far shore.

She unfastened her seat belt and watched him. "Matt, I've always been good with people. I can cut through the bull and see what a man or a woman is really all about. Tonight I realized that you're a lot more than a buyer. But I don't think you're part of the law. It's a lot of strange sensations, really."

"If you thought that, why didn't you turn me over to the Red Sticks?"

She looked up quickly when he used the term. "Yes, you

would know about them, if you're doing your homework on the organizations in Chinatown that deal drugs. First, let me get started right. My whole name is Linette Liu. I'm not going to tell those I work for my feelings about you. You're in no danger from me. Do you understand?''

"Yes. I understand and I'm patient. You can talk all night if you want to. I'm a good listener."

She grinned and some of the tension eased.

"Good, because I'm a talker. I'll do nothing to get you in trouble." She looked out the side window with her back to him a moment. Then she turned around and stared at his eyes. "Oh damn, I am probably signing my own death warrant. I want out. I'll tell you everything I know if you help me get out."

Her face was so striking, the expression so worried, so troubled, so confused, that it fascinated him.

Hawke nodded. "Of course I'll help you anyway I can. But if I could make a suggestion. You're talking like these people you work with have been known to kill traitors. My best advice would be that you're out now, stay out, never go back. Let me help you."

A look of great relief flooded her face. She leaned over and hugged him. She kissed his cheek and then sat back, more composed now, more sure of herself.

"I have to give you the whole program, the workup, the entire story." She smiled. "Sure you have time?"

"I'd say another sixty years, if I'm lucky."

Lin laughed. He was glad to hear her relaxing a little.

"Matt, I'm a native of Manhattan; in fact, I've never been out of the city of New York, never in my life. My parents were poor, we scraped along, and they were so honest it hurt. I got through the eighth grade on guts alone. Once I wore the same blouse and skirt to school every day for three months. I was teased without stopping. I started hitting the teasers, and then I found a razor blade, the single edge kind with a back you can hold.

"One day I cut up three girls who teased me, and nobody ever talked to me after that. They were afraid to. I learned a lot that year. Then a boy I liked started doing drugs, and before I knew it I went from pot to coke and on into heroin.

"In six months I was at a hundred dollars a day. My boyfriend was at almost two hundred. I started doing tricks on the street to pay for my fixes. Then Teddy, my friend, died in a robbery and I was alone. I'd run away from home when my father found out I was on drugs and whipped me.

"So I had nobody. By the time I was fifteen I was living on the streets and so dirty and awful looking that I couldn't even sell myself. Then I heard about a man who was supposed to help girls like me.

"I talked to him and he said he would get me cleaned up and give me a fancy dress and two or three fixes a day. All I had to do was look pretty.

"Sounded phony. I'd been on the streets for almost a year. I knew every scam, every line, every sad story in the book, and I had used all of them. But I was down and out. I couldn't lose. He took me to a place and they fixed me up fancy. A bubble bath and shampoo and gave me new nails and eyebrows. A woman spent an hour on my makeup, and another one spent two hours on my hair. When I came out of there I didn't know myself.

"They had me sign some kind of a paper, and then an hour later I found out what they were really doing."

She looked out the window again and shivered. Hawke sat and waited. This would all tie together sooner or later, he hoped.

"So, Matt, I had taken the bait. I was hooked by them, and they knew exactly what to do with me. It was a smaller operation than it is now, but about the same system.

"They took me into a room on a grand old-world Chinese throne chair. It's inlaid with gold leaf. The pillows, the fabrics are all woven with actual gold thread. I've heard that the chair itself is worth almost a million dollars.

"They gave me the most fabulous dress I've ever seen. It was a combination of traditional Chinese and modern and must have cost thousands. One woman spent two hours fitting it on me, sewing and pinning and making it exactly right.

"Then they put me in the chair and let me sit there a minute. A man came in and told me what I had to do. He said if I refused, I would be stripped, beaten up, given back my same clothes, and dropped in some alley where I'd quickly die of an overdose.

"I was much younger then. I had been at the absolute bottom. Suicide had seemed like a good idea for a long time. This was not so bad. I had a six-to-one chance to live. So I said, what the hell, I'd give it a try.

"They brought in four men to carry the throne chair, and we went through big doors into a dimly lighted room. I knew there were a lot of men there. That didn't bother me. I knew they were going to bet whether I lived or died, and that didn't bother me either. I'd had another fix and I was ready for anything.

"When the room quieted it meant the betting was over. I don't even remember the odds. The men bet whether I lived or died. I remember thinking that I'd never seen so much money in my life. About fifty thousand dollars had been bet that time.

"The head man on the game went through a little ceremony of taking out a silver revolver and showing everyone that the cylinders were empty. He put in one silver bullet, closed the cylinder, and spun it. Then he gave it to me.

"I had been told to push the little button halfway and spin the cylinder. I did. I decided that I was going to die anyway. It might as well be this way as by getting beaten to death. I did it so quickly some of the men almost missed it. When the cylinder came to a stop, I put the muzzle of the weapon to the side of my head and pulled the trigger. The hammer fell on an empty cylinder.

"I had won. I was still alive."

"Lin, is that how the girls I read about in the paper died? They played the same game, only they lost?"

She nodded.

When she looked over, there were tears in her eyes. "Not a very nice story so far, is it? But I had won. I also won all the heroin fixes I needed, but they controlled it. I was taken to a beautiful set of rooms and had TV and records, all the food and drink I wanted. Nothing was too good for me. Nobody forced me to have sex, but there was a boy about sixteen I could have if I wanted him.

"Then they told me that I would play the game again the next week. I screamed and scratched the man, but he knocked me down, punching me where it wouldn't show.

"He said there had been no agreement about what would happen if I won. That was now being told to me. If I won three times, there might, just might, be a place in their organization where I could work. The man was not promising anything."

She reached for a cigarette from her purse. "I know I shouldn't smoke, but I do." She lit it, opened the window, and blew the smoke outside.

"Well, I lived like a princess that week. They never used me sexually. I was happy and well cared for, for the first time in my life. Even though I knew it was a life that might last for only a week. The alternative was something I couldn't face.

"To make it a shorter story, I won the next two times in the throne chair as well, when the cylinder was empty under the hammer. They started calling me Lucky Lin. That was almost four years ago. A young Chinese man had just sneaked into the country from Canada and had taken over a large section of the old tong organization here. He ran the throne chair game.

"Nobody knew if he was working with the triads or not. The triads are hierarchical criminal societies with roots that go back almost a thousand years. They are now based in Hong Kong and Taiwan. Some people said he was tied in with 14K, the most powerful of all modern Chinese criminal societies. It's based in Hong Kong and controls the China White heroin trade.''

Hawke sat nailed to the seat. He hardly breathed, afraid that she would stop.

She glanced over at him. "I hope I'm not boring you."

Hawke laughed. "Not a chance. Please go on."

"The man's name was Dong Chu, and he ran the operation with the betting on my life and smuggled in a big part of the drugs in Chinatown. But he wanted much more. He visited me after the third win and shook his head. No one had ever won three times in a row before.

"Now he took me out of the rooms and gave me a new small apartment in a big building that he said he owned. Then he took me off heroin. He said nobody who worked for him could be a drug user. He did it cold turkey. I had a full time nurse, and two strong-arm men to stop me from killing myself or the nurse. It was the most terrible, unbearably painful experience I've ever been through. Hell couldn't be worse.

"But I made it, and the memory of that has kept me off everything since, except cigarettes. It took me six months. He came to see me every week.

"Then for a year I was his mistress. He brought in special tutors who taught me what I had missed in high school. He brought in computer experts who taught me about computers. I can program them, I can build them, I can create new ones, and repair them.

"Now I am one of about twenty people who work in Mister Chu's organization top-floor headquarters. Oh, he dropped the name Dong when somebody told him that was a slang word for penis in America. He forbade anyone to use that name again."

She looked at him. "Matt, that explosion at the cutting

house last night. Did you or your people have a hand in that?''

"Yes, Lin."

"Good!" she beamed.

"Lin, would you tell me the name of the group that you have been working with?''

"Yes. The name is well known. It's called New Control."

"Oh damn!" Hawke said. He watched her critically. He picked up her purse and opened it. There was no weapon inside.

"I'm not here to trap you or harm you, Matt."

"Then how do you explain how I got so lucky? I come to town with the intention of taking on the new Chinese operation that has dominated the Manhattan heroin trade, and you drop into my lap. I don't believe in coincidences."

"This is far from a coincidence. You met me, we did business. You came back, I was impressed by your style, your vibes. Does there have to be any more explanation? Good people can get lucky too. For my part, I was simply impressed by you. I knew that you were not a real buyer. Somehow I knew you were more than what you seemed to be. I took a chance on you and your friend being a plant from Mister Chu checking on me. I took the risk of you driving me right back to the Golden Dragon and turning me over to the headwaiter, who also owns the place. I'd be executed in an hour."

Hawke took his turn staring out the window at the New Jersey lights. What if everything she said were true? He would have the key to the whole outfit in the palm of his hand. He knew the man's name. He knew about the Golden Dragon. But he also could be setting Lin up for a terrible death.

"I'll make you an offer, Linette. You tell me everything I want to know about Mister Chu and the New Control. In exchange, I'll give you a large sum of money, fly you to Los Angeles, where you can melt into the Chinese community under a new name, and you'll be safe from Dong Chu forever."

She looked at her watch.

"I should be back in the building before two A.M. I must go back soon. There is someone there I'm trying to help, to protect. If I don't go back she'll be suspect too. I must get her out first."

"What about my offer? You'll tell me all I want to know?"

"Yes, yes, gladly, but first I have to take care of Ti. I can't just walk out on her."

"Tell me where the New Control headquarters are, Lin."

"Just as soon as I get Ti free and clear. Tomorrow for sure." She paused, then leaned over and kissed his lips. "I could make a phone call. Yes, that would cover for me and for Ti. Let's go somewhere so I can phone."

He kissed her back and she clung to him. "Lin, there's a phone in my hotel room."

She never said yes or no, just snuggled down beside him as he started the car and drove back to the hotel's parking garage. They took the elevator directly to his fifth floor room. Matt unlocked the door quickly and they slipped inside.

Lin went directly to the phone. She got an outside line and dialed, then spoke softly in Mandarin. She laughed and said something else, then made a second call that was short, crisp, and businesslike.

"This is Lin. Check me out. I'll be in the usual time tomorrow."

Lin put down the receiver and looked up at Hawke from where she sat on the bed. She pointed to the spot beside her and he sat down.

"Matt, I'm just so damn scared!" She leaned against him and his arm went around her. "Not of you, of that damned Chu. He's . . . he's so vicious, so single-minded. Everything is black and white with him, you're with him one hundred percent or you're a traitor.''

Hawke kissed her lips gently. She looked up and sighed, then kissed him back, and they both stretched out on the bed. She lay half on top of him and whispered in his ear.

"Ever since I saw you in the car two nights ago, I've been thinking about you. Wondering what it would be like with you."

He undressed her gently and as he did, she told him more and more about the New Control.

"Chu has half this town tied up on horse—no, more like three-quarters of it. That's not all, he's also into gambling, prostitution, and protection rackets. The whole thing is computerized. I set up most of it."

She helped him get the sleek black dress up and over her head.

"He's so organized." Linette watched him working at her bra and giggled. "Let me help; it's got a front fastener." She slid out of the bra.

"Where's the headquarters?"

"I really don't want to tell you until I'm sure I can get Ti out safely. Tomorrow night I'll tell you for sure. I do know about three big shipments of snow coming in. All within the next three days."

She took off Hawke's shirt and teased the black hairs on his chest. "When and where on the shipments. I want them."

She kissed him. "Are you telling me that you'll destroy the heroin when you get it?"

"Absolutely. The same way I did about a million dollars' worth out in Queens last night." He kissed her between her breasts, and she sighed and told him the time and place of the three shipments. He made quick notes on a pad of paper next to the telephone.

"Now, I think the time for talking is over for a while," Hawke said, his voice husky with the tension that was building. Lin kissed him hard and then rolled over on top of him. She laughed softly. "I really hoped this evening was not going to be wasted on just business talk."

Two hours later they lay on the bed, her head resting on his chest. She told him more about the New Control.

"A short time after Chu came here, he killed at least two of the most prominent men in Chinatown. He first asked for their cooperation to bring their tong organization in with him. They turned him down flat. Both men were killed and dismembered as a warning to the other tongs and to the twelve to thirteen other gangs and criminal outfits in Chinatown."

"Why didn't we get some beer or some cheese and crackers or something before we came up?" Hawke asked.

"Sexier things on our minds." Linette turned and propped her chin in her hands as she stared at his naked form. "You are really beautiful, like those nude statues. You should be a statue. I'll carve you someday. I wanted to be a painter—never quite made it."

"How did Chu freeze out the Mafia?"

"Slowly. They never saw him coming. He'd blow up or burn down a deli or a small grocery store where the pusher or the distributor worked. If some other Mafia outfit did it, the family would know where to hit and hit hard. But with a bunch of Chinamen running around, the old Mafia guys and the young businessmen types were thrown into panic. They tried to hit the Golden Dragon one night.

"Four of their best gunmen were knifed before they got to the front door. After that the Mafia just pulled back. They say they don't need the drug trade, that they're into legitimate businesses now."

Lin crawled under the covers and pulled them over her head. Her muffled voice came through.

"Come down here; I want to show you something," she said.

"I've already seen it," Hawke rasped.

"Not this way, you haven't."

He hadn't.

Then they slept. They woke just before dawn and made love again, softly, gently, and she cried in delight.

"Why can't it always be like this?" she asked.

"It can be for you. Safe and in Los Angeles or San Francisco. With your friend and straight and working at a good job in computers. You have valuable skills. Things are going to be great in San Francisco. For both you and Ti. Now we better get moving. Today's the day of that first shipment, and I've got some phone calls to make, some arrangements."

Hawke put Lin in a cab a block from his hotel, then went back and called Buzz. He woke up mad but mellowed in a rush.

"Hey, that Jasmine! Now there's a girl. We hit it off like an old-fashioned romance. I didn't even kiss her good-night, but I have plans for that young dancing lady. Big plans."

"Good, I've got plans for you. Busy today?"

"Not if you want to play Boy Scout."

"I do. Pick you up for breakfast, sports wear will be fine, nothing too flashy so we won't be remembered. We're meeting a Cadillac, a blue one with California plates."

"Which direction we heading?"

"North, so I'll pick you up and you can buy me breakfast. Hold the grits."

They ate breakfast about eight in a little restaurant on Broadway just past the park.

"Hey, you *can* get grits here," Buzz chortled. He wore chinos, a cotton flannel shirt, and a New York Mets baseball cap.

"Where did you get this tip, from Wong?"

Hawke grinned. "Not exactly, closer to the main man. I got it from Lin Liu."

"She let something slip?"

"She wants out. She's turned. We've got dates, times, and places for three shipments within the next three days. By tonight she's going to be free and clear of a guy called Mister Chu, the head honcho of the New Control."

Buzz whistled. "Sounds like you had a productive evening."

"True. You through with that French toast? We have an appointment to keep up in Van Cortlandt Park."

"Way up there? Two Hundred Fifty-fourth Street."

"The very same."

They got to the park more than an hour early. The meet was set for a rest room near the second entrance from the north end of the park.

"The Cadillac is a 1988 model, one of the big ones, light blue with California plates 2BJH-416. These guys have the horse hidden in the rear seat cushions of the Caddy. It came into Canada by boat from Thailand and down through U.S. customs at the border, where a new Caddy like this won't even get a sniff by the agents."

They took weapons out of the trunk in the deserted park. It was far too early for picnics and too warm for ice skating.

"Let's do this one quietly if we can. They won't be expecting any trouble. All we have to do is take out Chu's welcoming party and hope we can do that before the goods arrive."

Hawke screwed a silencer on his .45. It was the hush tube he carried with him whenever he could, even if he had to dump the .45. A silencer cut down the force and range of the autoloader, but the muffler out here in the park would be essential.

They took one grenade each and Buzz carried the Spas-12 wrapped in a newspaper as backup. They moved the Mustang out of sight of the rest room. Buzz waited inside the men's section, and Hawke was in some carefully clipped shrubbery at the near side of the parking area next to the rest rooms.

The meet was set for ten-thirty. Already it was ten-fifteen. As Hawke looked at his watch, a red Mazda pulled into the lot. It was the top of the line but certainly not armored. Two men inside sat a moment and waited. Then one of them got out.

He was Chinese. He walked toward the men's rest room while the other one waited. Hawke moved at once, floundering up from the bushes, using his drunk role, staggering onto the parking lot and taking a long time to see the car. When at last he focused on the car he stumbled toward it.

The driver jumped out. He held a two-foot-long baton painted red. The young man was almost as tall as Hawke.

"Get outta here you stupid lush!" the Red Stick snarled.

"Wh—What?" Hawke asked, evidently just becoming aware of the man's presence.

"I said, get the hell out of here. Shit, what a mess. How about five bucks to buy wine with?"

"Wine? Wine?" Hawke slurred the words. The Chinese snorted and reached in his pocket for his billfold. By that time Hawke was close enough. He leaped another two feet forward and kicked with his right foot as hard as he could, blasting his half boot into the man's crotch, turning his testicles into jelly and dumping the man on the blacktop. He screeched in pain and anger but had no power to reach for his weapon.

Hawke kicked the automatic away and dumped the screaming man in the back of the Mazda luxury car. He tied up the man and put a gag in his mouth. The keys were still in the Mazda. Hawke drove it down to the far end of the lot and left it there.

He ran back to his spot in the bushes and got his heartbeat settled down just as a light blue Caddy pulled into the park. The driver hesitated a moment at the entrance to the parking lot, then turned, came directly up to the rest room, and shut down the big engine.

The license plate checked: 2BJH-416. There were two

men in the car. They talked a minute, then one got out and walked into the bathroom.

Hawke didn't want to disable the Caddy. His drunk walk wouldn't work on this guy, who was protecting at least a six-million-dollar shipment of heroin. The muscle would shoot first and say he was sorry later. Hawke couldn't leave his position without being seen.

The Avenger took out the silenced .45 and jolted a round into the Cadillac's windshield. He was shooting at about an eighty-degree angle, and the round hit hard enough to star the safety glass before it glanced away.

The guy behind the wheel slid down and out the near door. There was no way the driver could tell where the round originated. He pulled a .45 and looked around. He was not Chinese.

"Over here!" Hawke shouted. The driver fired a shot at the bushes. Hawke sent three silenced .45 answers to the smuggler. The second one hit him in the chest, drove him back and down. He lifted the .45 to get off another shot, but his strength failed and the weapon fell from his hand.

Hawke came out of the bushes running, got to the men's room, and called from around the sturdy block screening wall.

"Buzz?"

There was no answer.

Hawke went around the corner with the .45 in both hands, ready to blast in any direction.

One man lay on the cement floor, his head at a strange angle to his body. Broken neck. The second man, the Caucasian who had just come in, lay on the floor with a gag in his mouth and his hands and feet tied together behind him. He glared at Hawke.

Hawke ran outside and heard the car coming. The Mustang pulled up beside the Caddy shielding the body on the ground.

"Figured I'd bring up a diversion with you pinned down,

but you didn't need it," Buzz said. "Damn! Just like old times."

"Yeah, the bad old times," Hawke said. "I'll drive the Caddy. Leave the garbage there on the ground. Figure we should get upstream near the water somewhere."

They drove both cars north from Dobbs Ferry along the Hudson River. Here and there would be an open spot with no houses or shopping centers next to the water. They stopped in one such area, and Hawke pulled out the rear seat of the Caddy. It was solidly packed with newspaper-wrapped packages of heroin. No springs, just the seat covering over the blocks of drugs.

"I figure all we have to do is take the Caddy here for a swim and the Hudson River will do the damage to the goods."

"Sounds reasonable. Back at the park I checked that Mazda. They didn't have any cash with them. This must be an all–New Control operation."

At that point a narrow path led down to a twenty-foot drop off to the Hudson River. Rough steps had been gouged in the cliff by eager young hands.

"Looks like as good a place as any," Hawke said. He started the Caddy, checked the glove compartment and then the trunk, but there was nothing of value. He put the Caddy into gear and aimed it down the incline toward the drop-off.

The car picked up speed in the fifty feet to the cliff, and when it went over, it nosed down and hit hard on the grille on the very edge of the shoreline, then toppled forward and splashed into the river. It floated a moment as the current moved it downstream. Then it sank slowly, drifting fifty feet before it vanished under the water.

"What the hell you guys doing?" a voice blasted at them from some low brush nearby.

They both turned, hands near their weapons.

A man stood and waved. "Best show I've had in days.

Damn, but that Cadillac made a splash. What's this all about?''

Hawke could see him plainly now, a knight of the road, a street person, a bum. Hawke walked over to him grinning.

"Little trick I'm playing on my old man. He's loaded, see, and he bought me this new Caddy, but I said I wanted a Porsche and he threw a fit. So I'm dumping the car where he won't never find it.''

Hawke stripped a bill off his roll. He handed it to the bum, who looked at it in surprise.

"Hey, no way. Nobody'll change a hundred for me. Would you? Got maybe a ten or a twenty?''

A half hour later they were on the Henry Hudson Parkway heading down toward Fifty-seventh Street.

"How much you figure we melted down back there?'' Buzz asked.

"Supposed to be a hundred pounds.''

"Another six million dollars' worth!'' Buzz looked at Hawke. "It ever get to you, dumping that much value? You could keep the shit and resell it and be a millionaire.''

"I already have more drug money than I know what to do with. Maybe on this next hit we make you'll see what I mean. Most drug sales are made for cash because nobody trusts nobody. Immature of them, I know. I've seen a dozen grocery sacks stuffed with hundred-dollar bills.

"If we have a chance we'll always save the cash. Cash money is never tainted. I gave two million dollars to a Catholic priest at a poor little place down in Colombia. Should have seen his face.''

"If you have any to spare . . .'' Buzz laughed. "Hell, then I'd have to figure out some way so it wouldn't show on my income tax. That could be more work than it would be worth.''

As they inched along in the Fifty-seventh Street traffic, Buzz had another question. "What's on for this afternoon?''

"Research.''

"Good, tonight I have a date. A late date, and we won't be in until morning."

"Jasmine?"

"Right. That's the best thing you've ever done for me."

"Good." He hit the horn and swept past a few belligerent pedestrians who know they own the Manhattan crosswalks.

"I've got a date tonight, too. I hope. If she shows up. She warned me not to go to the Golden Dragon again. One way or the other, I have to find Lin if she doesn't contact me."

By eight o'clock that evening, Lin Liu had not called. He had told her his hotel number. Hawke put the silenced .45 in his belt under a sport coat and headed toward the door. He had to find Lin!

CHAPTER
SIX

The three Chinese girls in the hallway about to pick the lock on his door surprised Hawke as much as they were surprised. He had just opened the door to leave. Hawke grabbed the hand reaching forward, jerked the girl inside, and slammed the heavy panel closed before the other two girls could move.

He jolted the inside woman against the wall, pulled the silenced Uzi from her hands, and pushed her to the floor. At the same time he flattened against the wall as silent .45 caliber rounds splintered through the door from the Uzi outside. The wood was thicker than it looked, and the rounds were spent by the time they penetrated the two inches.

He reached over and fixed the chain lock, then pushed the chair up against the door, all the time watching the girl on the floor. She wore black skintight pants and a black T-shirt. She seemed small and helpless lying there on the rug. Hawke had no doubts about her ability.

He dropped on top of her suddenly, forcing her back to the floor, his knee in the small of her back.

"No, that hurts!" she screeched.

"That was to let your friends know you're still alive," Hawke said. He grabbed the girl's left arm and pinned it behind her. Her right arm lay under her.

"Bring out your other arm or your head hits the floor hard!" Hawke growled. She brought out the hand and tried to slice him with the small blade. He chopped her wrist with the side of his hand and she screamed, dropping the knife.

"Who sent you?" he demanded.

There was no response. He grabbed a handful of black hair and slammed her head down on the carpet. The rug wasn't that thick here. Her head bounced off and she groaned.

"Who sent you?"

Again she didn't respond. He pulled a strip of plastic from his pocket. It was a small riot cuff that many police departments use. This one was only a quarter of an inch wide but tough enough to hold a pro football player on PCP. He pushed her wrists together and bound them with the plastic. The tighter he pulled it, the more notches engaged. It would come off only by being cut away.

Hawke helped her stand. She spat in his face. He wiped the fluid away and slapped her hard. Then he pushed her ahead of him and kicked away the chair. He made noise as he opened the door. First he peered out and saw no one. He pushed the girl out to the left down the hall, using her as a shield. He watched to the right.

He heard the chatter of high speed rounds from the left. Two slugs hit the girl and she sagged against him. He looked to the right and saw a figure dart out and lift a weapon. Hawke fired three times with his silenced .45. The reduced kick helped him keep on target, and the far shooter spun around, jolted off the wall before she sprawled dead in the hallway.

Hawke jumped back into his room before the gunwoman to the left could target him. He locked the door, pushed the chair against it, and ran to the window. He remembered thinking what an old hotel this was when he checked in. The windows even opened, and there was a metal fire escape. He threw his clothes and the dead girl's silenced Uzi subgun into his suitcase and stepped onto the fire escape. He saw no one.

Ten minutes later he was down the six flights of iron steps and catching a cab in the street.

A chilling calm settled over him. There were only three people who knew where he was. He knew they had found out about Lin Liu. If they discovered she wanted to leave, they would question her, brutally. No one could withstand that kind of torture.

The cabby looked at him.

"Meter's running, Mack."

"Yeah, uptown about ten more blocks to a small hotel. Take your pick. You bird-dogging for anybody?"

"There aren't that many tourists down here, Mack."

The hotel where he checked in was smaller but taller— nine stories, but it looked like it was only about twenty feet wide. He used a different name and left his gear in his room. Now he had to reclaim his rented Mustang and his vital ordnance. By this time there would be help for the one Chinese woman hit man who tried for him in his hotel room. Too much Red Stick help probably. If they knew his hotel, they knew he had a car and where it was parked.

The advantage was his. He'd wait until dark, go in the street door, heist his tools, and leave the car there. To backstop the plan, he used the phone in his room and rented a car. For an extra twenty dollars they agreed to deliver it to the street in front of the Pettibone Hotel on East Twenty-sixth.

The car arrived and he phoned Buzz at his apartment. He was in. They laid out the parameters for the mission the next morning. Then he told Buzz about his visitors.

"Three women hit men? Bizarre. Next they'll be using kids. Yeah, I got the signals. A light tan Mustang with a large number two painted on the roof. Hope it don't rain. Yeah. You take it easy. You want some help picking up the goods at the airport?"

"None needed. Got a plan. I'll see you tomorrow about noon at that LZ."

"Right. Wish we had some radio connect, but we'll make it. Mustang, light tan with a number two on the top. Won't be many of those around. Hey, don't tell me where your new hotel is. That way no problems. You want me, call."

"Right. I'm outta here."

Hawke stopped at a tobacco store and found what he wanted—a small bottle of lighter fluid, the kind you used to use to fill up old-fashioned lighters. It was five ounces and had a screw top. Just right.

He parked his newly rented tan Mustang a block from his former hotel and walked around until it was dark, then slid in the street door of the garage. He hid behind cars for fifteen minutes until he got the layout. There were four killers waiting for him. Two at the far end. One near his old Mustang and another one who had moved to the exit door.

The street man would be first. Hawke came up behind the Red Stick so quietly, the tall Chinese with a .45 in his right fist never heard him until the last moment, when Hawke's own silenced .45 chugged softly and the stick man went down with a head shot.

Hawke worked his way between cars until he was directly behind the man watching his old Mustang. He worked forward as far as he could and made it within jumping distance, and still the man didn't know he was there. The guy was too dumb to live.

Hawke ran forward three steps, saw the surprised man turn, then Hawke brought the butt of his .45 down hard on the Red Stick's head. He heard his skull crack, and the guard went down in a heap, dead before he found concrete.

Hawke opened the trunk of the Mustang without a sound, put the guns, ammo, and explosives all in one cardboard box, then lifted it out and eased the trunk lid down but didn't latch it. Everything fit nicely in the one box except the Spas-12, whose muzzle jutted out two inches.

Hawke took out the bottle of lighter fluid, unscrewed the top, and pushed in the top half of one of his handkerchiefs he had cut in two. He balled it until it served as a stopper, then tipped the little bottle upside down until it saturated the three inches of white cloth. He had a small lighter ready as he walked between cars toward the street entrance.

The guards were looking for a drive-out. He had the advantage. He put the box down behind a car two over from the street exit and made sure where the guards were. One had moved closer to the door, in the open next to a concrete pillar.

Just right, Hawke figured. He snapped the lighter, lit the end of the lighter-fluid-soaked cloth, lifted up, and in one move threw the small bottle at the concrete post beside the Red Stick guard.

The wick flickered as it sailed through the air.

Somebody bellowed out a warning.

The bottle hit the concrete, shattered, and sprayed burning lighter fluid across the waist and legs of the guard.

As soon as he threw the bottle, Hawke grabbed the box and walked toward the exit. When the bottle shattered, he ran. There was no pistol fire. He was out the driveway, to the street, and down the block to his car without a scratch or a tail.

Hawke slid into the driver's seat, pushed the box onto the passenger's side and drove toward his new hotel on Twenty-sixth. This one didn't have a garage, which meant his rig would be on the street and liable to Manhattan search and rescue thieves. They searched for anything they could rescue off a car and sold it.

He carried the box of weapons up to his room and slid it under the bed. Then he added the big silenced Uzi submachine gun to his treasures. It was large and heavy, but damned effective.

Hawke took the subway to Mott Street and got off in the middle of Chinatown. He had put on a floppy hat pulled down low and an old pair of blue jeans, sneakers, and a used shirt he had bought on Canal Street. It had two army patches on one arm and a faded place on the other one that showed sergeant stripes had once been sewn there. He let the shirt hang outside the jeans.

At a corner phone booth, Hawke dialed the Golden Dragon. He asked for the headwaiter and then for Lin Liu.

"I'm sorry, Miss Liu hasn't come in yet tonight. I don't expect her much before eleven."

"Thanks." He hung up. He phoned David Wong. The banker said he had no news.

"My contact in Group Forty-one thought it strange that the same day he gave me the address of that suspected cutting house, it got blown up and six people were killed."

"Hope you told him it was a real tragedy, that gas explosion. Gas is a terrible threat to people around here."

"I tried but he didn't buy it. He wants to meet you."

"Not a chance. I'm allergic to DEA people. Tell him that. I'm learning more about this New Control outfit. They have a Russian roulette kind of game, and men bet on whether the subject lives or dies. I'm almost certain that's the kind of game they had Shensi play the night she died. I'd know a lot more, but my contact inside the New Control might have been discovered."

"That would be tragic."

"True. I want you to be sure to stay well away from this area. No contact at all with those people."

"But they did kill my sister."

"Yes, but concentrate now on keeping yourself and your other sister alive. Are you reading me, David?"

"Reluctantly. I wish there was more I could do."

"Right now, go to work, see a movie, have a date, and let me handle the rest of it."

That night Hawke tried three more times to contact Lin Liu at the Golden Dragon. Each time someone told him that she was not expected in that evening, that he should call tomorrow night.

Hawke was sure that they had found out about Lin Liu. Damn!

Hawke prowled Chinatown, saw a pusher selling heroin on the street, and beat the man into the gutter and trashed his papers of heroin. He knew he was taking his anger at New Control out on the pusher, but he didn't care.

He found a second man selling, and the young Chinese got away only because he dove into his car. Hawke put a silenced .45 round through the back window as the car raced up the block, its back tires squealing on the blacktop.

Matthew Hawke was so angry that night that he knew he wouldn't be able to sleep. He finally went back to his room about two A.M. He watched a movie for a while, but all the time he heard Lin Liu telling him about how brutal and deadly the New Control enforcers were. Now he was sure they had Lin Liu, and he didn't even know where their headquarters were.

He dropped off to sleep about four A.M. with the TV set still on.

Hours later, "Good Morning, America," the early TV show, woke him. He brushed his teeth twice, but the ugly, cancerous taste of death lingered in his mouth.

Today he would pay them back a little bit for what he was sure Lin Liu was suffering.

He carried his cardboard box of goods down to the sidewalk and started toward his car. Three young street toughs, evidently still up after a wild night, blocked the sidewalk.

"What's in the box, man?" one asked. He had a skull and crossbones drawn in ink on his forehead. He was white, about eighteen and six-two.

Hawke ignored him.

"We talking to you, honkie!" a black kid near the same height, but no so well built, jawed at Hawke.

"An automatic shotgun, five pounds of plastic explosive, and six grenades—want me to use one?"

"You jiving me, man!" the black said. The other, a smaller white boy who was younger, pulled at the pair.

"Let's get out of here; that shit might explode!"

Hawke lifted from the box his .45, which still had the silencer on it, and aimed it right between the eyes of the white kid.

"You want a new asshole up this high, rectum face, or are you going to be a nice little asshole and move to one side and let a man walk down the street?"

"Christ, we just kidding you!" the black said. He jumped into the street.

"It's a fake," the white kid snarled. Three garbage cans sat on the sidewalk waiting for pickup. Hawke turned and fired once into the cans, and in a flick of his arm the weapon centered on the white kid's belly.

"Any more dumb remarks?" Hawke asked.

The three ran into the street and hurried down the black-top in the other direction.

Twenty feet down, the owner of a small deli was out sweeping the sidewalk in front of his store. He waved at Hawke.

"Be glad to have you stop by every morning," he said. "Them three been messing in my face for a week."

"They won't be back," Hawke said. He put the box down and bought a cup of coffee and a cheese Danish.

"What's really in the box?" the deli owner asked, making change for a ten for Hawke.

"Just what I said." He reached into the box and pulled out one of the old-style grenades.

"Be damned," the deli owner rasped. "Live?"

"Until it goes off." Hawke finished the Danish and the coffee, thanked the man, and went on down to his car. The hubcaps were gone. Hawke didn't realize that kids stole hubcaps anymore.

He opened a small jar of watercolor black paint and used a half-inch-wide brush to paint a 2 on top of his car. The number was three feet high and three inches wide. The water-based paint dried immediately. Any chopper in the sky should be able to see it. He put a gallon of water he had recently bought in the front seat, in case he needed a fast wash job, and pulled out into traffic.

It took him an hour and a half to drive out to Kennedy Airport. He wasn't sure of the way and his map was little help, but he found it. He drove around it, found the air express center and parked, watching the whole operation.

International flights came into one area. That would help. Lin said it was an art shipment from Tokyo on Japan Air Lines. Hawke walked around the international flight area and talked with one of the freight handlers.

"Yeah, we got two planes set to come in soon from Tokyo, a JAL and a Pan Am."

"Must have customs men here," Hawke said.

"Yeah, they slow things down. Look over some stuff good, some they just crack a seal or two. Never can tell. Depends who's on duty."

The worker hurried off to some task. Lin said the shipment would be picked up by a stretched Ford van painted red. No markings on it except a 333 on both back doors and on the front doors.

That he could find. The Chinese lucky numbers.

A half hour later he saw the JAL plane land and taxi up to

the terminal. It was an all-freight flight and disgorged a
warehouse full of goods.

A red Ford van slid into a parking spot reserved for "Air
Express Pickup," and two Chinese men stepped out. One of
them talked to an airport worker, who brought somebody
else, and soon a fold of a dozen bills changed hands almost
out of sight, and the goods for the red van were put through
inspection first.

One of the customs men had seen the transaction, and he
scowled. The air freight boxes were cardboard, four feet
square, and about six inches wide. ORIGINAL OIL PAINTINGS
was printed on the outside.

The customs man opened one of the boxes and took out
the paintings. There were two, face to face in frames, and
around the paintings were cushioning material in sturdy
burlap bags, made so it would absorb the pressure of the
sliding and jolting of the picture frames without hurting
them.

The inspector dug all the way to the bottom, brought out
one of the burlap bags and looked at it, then checked the
paintings. He snorted. "Damn things aren't worth the two
hundred each listed on the manifest. Somebody is getting
rooked." He put a sticker on one of the boxes, gave seven
more to a helper who stickered the other boxes, and they
were trucked to the dock. There they were carefully stowed
in the red Ford 333 van.

This had to be it, Hawke decided. Imported art from
Tokyo, JAL carrier, red pickup, and the 333 lucky Chinese
numbers. He drifted out to his Mustang. The number on the
roof was intact. He looked at his map and decided where he
would try to make his move. The van was heavier than his
rig, so he had to be positive and demanding in his try.

Hawke had the Mustang's engine running and shortly
tailed the red van out of the air express area onto the exit
lanes and up the 687 Van Wyck Expressway knifing toward
Queens and Manhattan.

At the Rockaway Boulevard offramp, the van was hugging the right-hand lane. Evidently the driver had strict instructions not to exceed the speed limit and risk getting stopped by the cops. As the offramp came up, Hawke pulled alongside the red van, then swung away and slammed back toward the van. The Mustang crashed into the larger rig, jolting it sideways.

The driver had not seen the Mustang coming, and the van angled into the offramp before the driver could correct. Hawke saw an angry face in the window as he slid in behind the truck, which turned north onto Rockaway Boulevard, spurted ahead and then angled into the big unused parking lot at Aqueduct racetrack. Good, Hawke thought. He had not been able to give his air support an exact LZ. This was deserted, ideal.

Hawke followed them. The red rig stopped and Hawke pulled up nearby. The driver came boiling out of the truck holding a ten-inch crescent. Before Hawke got out of the car the other driver smashed the Mustang's windshield with the wrench.

"Bastard! What the hell you doing? Don't you look where you're going?" He lifted the wrench again and Hawke shot the Red Stick man through the heart with the silenced autoloader. He fell over the Mustang's fender and never moved.

Hawke carried the .45 behind him as he walked over to the open door on the van. The second man in the small truck looked out.

"I think your buddy over here had a heart attack or something," Hawke said.

"Christ, what next?" the young man bellowed and ran over to the Mustang. He touched his buddy's shoulder and he slid off the fender, leaving a long streak of blood.

The Red Stick had drawn his .38 revolver when Hawke put a .45 round squarely in his throat. A second silenced shot drilled into his chest. He surged backward and sprawled next to his dead partner on the blacktop.

Hawke heard a chopper, to the left and north. It came closer, circled, then set down twenty yards away. Hawke had just dumped the two bodies into the Mustang and taken out his box of weapons when he saw Buzz step out of the helicopter and walk toward him.

It took them fifteen minutes to slice open the cardboard boxes and pull out the burlap sacks from the eight boxes of art. Hawke figured the "packing" had to be the heroin. It was. They backed the red van up to the chopper and loaded the forty-eight bags of heroin into the rig, then the box of weapons, and climbed in.

A racetrack security pickup rolled away from the main building to the north and headed for the chopper. Long before it got there and the driver could read any of the bird's ID numbers, the chopper lifted off and Buzz slanted away toward Jamaica Bay, due south.

"What's this—a slice and drop mission?" Buzz asked. "I had a hell of a time finding you. That number on the roof was a great idea."

Hawke pulled out his folding pocket knife and sliced open the heavy burlap for a better look. Inside was a plastic liner filled with heroin.

"So we have to slice open each one, or the natives will be beachcombing heroin for dinner," Hawke said.

It took them twenty minutes of flying to get rid of all forty-eight sacks of heroin. They had flown out across Rockaway Beach and swung over the Atlantic by the time Hawke had the last bag sliced open and dumped out the door.

"Home, James," Hawke said.

"You smash up another car?" Buzz asked. "Man, nobody is going to rent a car to you again."

"That's why I signed for that one in your name." Hawke brayed and laughed at Buzz's expression.

They landed back at the chopper port on the Hudson River frontage, and Hawke carried his box of arms and explosives out to the parking lot. Buzz paid the rest of the bill, got back his pilot and driver's licenses and pointed to a new Porsche.

"You do have one," Hawke said, sliding into the rig.

"True, just transportation."

"Nice way to go. You going to drive me over to my hotel, or do you know where we can talk with one of the tong leaders in town? They do still have the tongs here, don't they?"

"Sure, there are some around. But by now they are all old men, and their power is almost nil. They have no push, no value, control almost nothing. Most of the men are seventy to eighty years old, and they get together on Thursdays to play mah-jongg for pennies."

"Scratch the visit to the tongs. We still have one more hit at a shit shipment, tomorrow. You game?"

"Why not?"

"It's a Piper Comanche supposedly bringing in another one hundred pounds of horse up in New Jersey. Can we get the same chopper for tomorrow?"

"Told the guy we might need it. We're reserved."

"Good, now let me off a block from my hotel and you can get in to work and earn this Porsche."

Twenty minutes later Hawke walked into his hotel with the box of arms. There was no note for him in his room box. Good—no one was supposed to know he was here. He had some phone calls to make, and he had to find Lin Liu!

Mister Chu drummed his fingers on the luxurious stretch limo's writing desk, which swung down from the side. He was not in the mood to do any work. Too many things had been going wrong. Why? Why? His organization seemed as solid as ever.

First the Cadillac shipment from Canada went sour and he

lost two men and the one hundred pounds. Then just today the art air shipment of one hundred pounds of horse was lost along with two good men. How could this happen? Where did this white bastard come from who shot up his princesses? Why?

He knew but he refused to admit it. There had to be a traitor high up in his top operational team. Someone he had trusted, whom he had counted on for loyalty and for the functioning of New Control.

Whoever it was would pay. He had some candidates; he just wasn't sure which one it was yet. Three of them. One of them would admit it before long.

The big car stopped in a small street deep in Chinatown. The one princess he had left hurried out of the big car and checked the street both ways, then opened the door and led him into a small food store. It was no more than a corner market, and the small Chinese man who ran it bowed low as the delegation trooped inside.

The thin old man said something, but Mister Chu brushed him aside and walked through a curtain into a back room. He continued into another room that was living quarters, and down steps into a basement. Two doors later he came into a brightly lighted room with twelve old Chinese men playing mah-jongg at a teakwood and ivory table.

They all stood at once.

Hu Chao came forward, bowed, and smiled up at the taller young man.

"Mister Chu. We have heard much about you. This is your first visit to our humble and worthless meeting."

"Worthless is right," Chu snapped. He waved his hand, and two Red Sticks swept the other old men from the room, rushing them out two doors until only Mister Chu and Hu Chao remained.

The older man motioned to chairs beside the table and both sat down.

"Hu Chao, I have come to talk to you about the tongs. I

know of twelve that remain in the city. I want all of you to come under my control, to work through me. With this added strength and support of the people, we will truly control every aspect of life in Chinatown and wherever our people live.''

''Would you have some green tea?'' Hu Chao asked. He poured into a small handleless cup and lifted it toward Mister Chu. The New Control leader slapped it out of his hand, and the delicate cup shattered when it hit the floor.

''I said I want you and the other tongs to join my organization!'' Mister Chu bellowed.

''Mister Chu. There may be a chance you do not understand our small groups, which were once powerful, which once ran every vice and activity in Chinatown. We are now old; some say we are toothless. We are no longer dragons that roar and spit fire from our mouths.

''We are simple people who have lived long, and now hope only to have our small pleasures and to take joy in our expanded families.''

He poured a second cup of green tea and sipped it.

''We no longer have any of the power that you seek. We cannot sway the people, or threaten them, or control them. A little gentle influence is all we have left.''

Mister Chu grew increasingly irritated with the long speech. He burst in at the end of it.

''Then come join us with that influence. We will give you some of the power you have lost. We will help make your old age more meaningful.''

The ancient Chinese man stroked long chin whiskers and rubbed at watery eyes. Slowly he shook his head.

''Mister Chu, we play games on Thursday. We are not criminals. We do not threaten and murder. We do not deal in drugs or prostitution. We are simple old men living in the past.''

Mister Chu jumped up from the table, knocking over the

heavy chair. He shouted several words in Chinese and two of the Red Sticks rushed into the room, guns raised.

He said something else, softly, and one of the men darted out the door. He came back a moment later with a heavy long blade resembling a machete more than a war ax. The blade was two feet long and six inches wide, nearly half an inch thick at the top, slanting down into a razor sharp blade.

"Hu Chao, you refuse to join us?"

"We have nothing to offer..."

"You refuse to work with us?"

"We are not in the fields that would..."

"You are not with me, therefore you are against me." He took the big machete from the Red Stick and hefted it."

"You know what this is, Hu Chao?"

"Yes. An executioner's ax, dating from one of the early dynasties. A rare and valuable treasure owned by our ancestors."

"It also is still able to serve its function." Without warning, Mister Chu swung the heavy weapon downward. He had aimed at the old man's head, but the ancient one had time to slip to the side.

The sturdy weapon came down instead on the top of Hu Chao's shoulder, broke the bones there, sliced downward, and severed his left arm from his body. Chao screamed and fell unconscious to the left, against the table.

Mister Chu breathed quickly from the exertion but lifted the executioner's ax again and powered it down, decapitating the old tong leader. His head rolled onto the polished table and lay still, leaving a trail of draining blood.

The New Control leader barked orders in Chinese, and the two Red Sticks jumped forward and pushed the body of Hu Chao on the table, where it lay in three pieces.

Mister Chu looked at it.

"Three is a lucky number; we can't leave him that way. It must be in four parts—four, the death number!" He swung the heavy ax again from high overhead directly down on the corpse's torso.

With one slashing blow the ax bit through bone, muscle, and flesh to chop the slender body in half. Now the old man lay in four parts.

"Enough!" he said, panting from the exertion. "The tongs now know that they are totally finished in Chinatown. Spread the word that this is their only warning. The New Control has taken over and will guide and rule and direct everything that happens here!"

CHAPTER
SEVEN

In his hotel room, Hawke changed clothes into his street person attire, old and sloppy pants and shirt and a wide brimmed hat he pulled low to help hide his face. He tried to call David Wong at the bank, but he was out. He left a message that he had called using the name Matt.

Then he roamed around Chinatown, trying to find a crack in the New Control armor.

Instead he came up against the brick walls of a closed community. If he wanted to buy or shop, he was allowed. But he could move no farther. No one would talk to him about any phase of crime. Once when he mentioned New Control, he was hustled out of the small store and pushed down the street.

Everyone was frightened. No one would talk. His Caucasian features labeled him at once as an outsider, a possible cop, and one to be mistrusted.

At last he phoned David Wong again at the bank. He was in. He told him he had moved to a new hotel.

"Yeah, I tried to call you a couple of times. My DEA

friend is getting insistent. He's about ready to arrest me if I don't let him see you.''

"Don't let him give you a bad time. Hell, maybe after tomorrow. Tell him this is my busy time. I'll find a spot for him in the next couple of days.''

"Great, I'll get him off my back. Reason I called you is I got a strange note today. One of the clerks brought it over to me. When she tried to point out the man who had left it, he had already gone. She said only that he was a tall Chinese man about twenty-five.''

"One of them?''

"My guess. The note said if I knew how to contact the white guy who had been bothering Lin Liu, I should tell him to come to the Uptown side of Fourteenth Street and Broadway subway station about eight-thirty tonight. The note says this bohunk has some news from Lin for you.''

"I bet. I think Mister Chu has already grabbed Lin. Three women tried to gun me down in my old hotel. Chu couldn't find out where I was anywhere else.''

"So it's a trap.''

"Yeah, but I'll have to show up one way or the other. I have some time to think it through. Keep close tabs on Jasmine for the next couple of days. It also wouldn't hurt if you stayed with friends or in a hotel.''

"Hey, they can't have anything against me.''

"They wouldn't need to. If you can contact me, you're a danger to them. So be careful.''

"Yeah, I will. We'll set something up with the DEA guy later. I've got a customer.''

They said good-bye and Hawke watched the street. He put on large reflectorized sunglasses and walked past the Golden Dragon. It was open but he wasn't going in. Nothing looked any different. He was sure Lin Liu would never see the place again. Dammit! He slammed his hand into the side of a building and felt the hurt travel up his arm and all the way into his brain. He wanted it to hurt, because he figured that Lin was hurting even worse.

Under the floppy shirt he felt the .45 pushing against his skin. It was comforting. He had thirteen little backups down there. That would pull a lot of weight with some Red Sticks. It had to be them on the subway meet. But on the other hand, there was an outside chance that Lin could have found a way to get a note to him.

He had to check it out.

At eight-thirty that night he arrived at the subway platform at Fourteenth and Broadway and got off. It was a mixed neighborhood, and in five minutes he heard five different languages and saw every color and shade of person living on Manhattan. Two local trains came and left.

There were never more than half a dozen people on the platform. Then a swarm of people clamored down the stairs. They were mostly young men, with a few women. A gang with jackets—they were all Chinese. They looked up and down the platform, then began talking to each person waiting.

Hawke had surveyed the terrain as soon as he came down. There was a double track here. The platform was about two hundred feet long with one entrance/exit. On the far end, the platform stopped in the black hole of the tunnel heading downtown.

Closest to him, the platform terminated fifty feet north and continued only with another dark tunnel heading uptown. The tracks had three rails—the gleaming third rail carrying the electricity. More than one commuter had jumped, fallen, or been pushed onto that deadly piece of electrified steel and had died immediately.

Gangs also like to crowd their victim to the very edge of the platform and, just as an express whistles through, push the person in front of the flashing rapid transit car.

So many ways to die.

The gang worked closer. One of the younger kids ran

ahead and stopped in front of Hawke, who still had on the shades.

"Hey man, you always wear them at night?" the young Chinese boy asked.

"Your fly's open," Hawke snorted.

The boy checked, growled. He turned to his buddies. "We got a smart fuck up here."

Two more young men hurried up. This pair was larger, and Hawke saw that one of them twirled a red baton on a leather strap around his wrist.

Hawke eased the .45 out of his belt and held it just under the floppy shirt.

He showed it. "Turn around and run," Hawke spat. "Or you're soaking up lead, assholes!"

The young kid bolted away. The other two laughed. "You use that in here and you're dead. We got more manpower than you got bullets, and we all high, man. We so high flying we don't even remember what bullets do. You want to start shooting?"

They were so close now that they could lunge at him. He couldn't shoot them all down.

Hawke jumped off the platform, careful to miss the third rail, and ran toward the black tunnel heading uptown.

There were shouts then and a quick conference by the Red Sticks. Half a dozen of the gang ran for the entrance stairs. Six of the larger ones jumped down into the tracks and started after Hawke.

He came to the dark hole and as soon as he vanished into it, he fired a shot into the rock wall. The chasers behind him stopped, conferred again as Hawke got used to the semi-darkness, and ran forward. There was enough light so he could avoid stepping on the electrified rail. Every so often a dim bulb marked the tracks.

He saw three-foot-deep niches cut into the rock wall here and there along the two-train-wide tunnel.

Down the tracks he heard a train coming. It stopped at the

station behind and Hawke kept running. He could jump to the tracks on the other side to get out of the way. Then he heard a train coming from ahead of him. What the hell now? It had to be on the other tracks, the downtown route.

He checked the niches on the side as he ran. They were about every fifty feet or so. He heard the train start up behind him and searched for another dug-out spot in the tunnel wall. He found it, wedged in beside some pipes and conduit, and turned his face away as the headlight glared in the black tunnel behind him.

He never moved as the train came forward. He heard shouts in back of him from the six gang members. Then the grinding, rattling roar of the train was on him, and he heard two chilling screams behind him along the tracks.

Some of the chasers didn't find a spot off the tracks, or they hit the third rail.

A sucking, slashing rush of air buffeted him for twenty seconds, then the careening, rattling train was past. At once Hawke jumped back to the tracks and ran forward. His eyes were more adjusted now. How far was it to the next stop? He couldn't remember.

Behind him he heard wails and screams.

Hawke ran on, being certain where the third rail lay.

The cries behind him faded.

Far ahead he saw a pinpoint of new light.

Ten minutes later he arrived at a spot where he could see the station. There were eight of the Chinese gang near his end of the station platform.

How in hell could he get past them? Wait for an incoming train, one disgorging a whole bunch of people. Might work.

He watched for five minutes. A train whistled by on the other track going downtown. He huddled in an equipment niche and kept out of sight.

Someone with the gang's denim-jacket colors ran down the steps, called to the gang members, and hurried to them. They all bellowed in rage and five of them ran back up the steps. The three who were left carried the red batons, Red Sticks from the New Control.

Five minutes later a train rattled up from the south. It pulled into the station and people surged out. Hawke tried to time it exactly. He crept along bent over to the very end of the platform, then jumped up and ran behind a cluster of four children around a pair of adults.

"It's him!" one of the Red Sticks shouted. Hawke powered forward toward the steps. One of the gang members stood in front of him. He swung the baton.

Hawke caught it with his hand, yanked forward, and pulled the slender young man into his upraised knee, which then crashed into his belly. The Red Stick screeched, dropped to the platform, and vomited.

One of the other two stopped to help him; the third ran on. Hawke was up one flight of concrete steps when he heard the man close behind him. He whirled, kicked out. His foot connected solidly with the Red Stick man, who looked down, concentrating on the steps. His head snapped back and he lost his balance, falling and sprawling down the twelve steps to the next landing.

Somebody screamed below him.

Hawke ran up the rest of the steps to the street and jogged down half a block. No one followed him.

So much for checking out the note from Lin Liu. He closed his eyes for a moment in a silent prayer to all the gods of the universe that she was still safe. He walked slowly back to his hotel on Twenty-sixth Street. He'd have to rent one more car, under another name. He was running out of identification. He'd need to get some more made. Three sets were usually enough.

At the hotel he looked in his box and asked for the key that they told him to leave. There were no messages. The clerk, with the same hollow-eyed look as usual, gave Hawke his key, and he went up the elevator to the ninth floor.

When he opened the door and pushed it inward, he sensed something was wrong, but by then it was too late.

"Don't move," a voice said from the darkness. Someone behind him turned on the light switch, and he stared into the muzzle of a .38 Police Special. The man holding it looked Irish. At least he wasn't Chinese.

Hawke glanced behind when someone there closed the door. This one was Chinese. Both men wore suits. Oh damn.

"Welcome to the DEA convention," Hawke said. "You can put away the hardware; I'm not about to shoot you."

The man holding the gun kept it and eased up from the room's one chair. He was about forty, clean shaven, with sharp blue eyes.

"Interesting collection we found in the box under your bed."

"A man has to have some tools to work with."

"Especially in your line of work," the gun wielder said. He flipped a newspaper to Hawke, who saw a picture of the van and Mustang in the racetrack parking lot, with half a dozen police swarming around it.

"You do good work, have to give you that. I heard a first name that sounds right—Matt. Could that be for Matthew?"

"Why should I help you in your interrogation?"

"Because if you don't I've got you on illegal arms, illegal explosives, hand grenades, and a dozen other charges, including packing that .45 in your waistband without a county license. Good enough for starters?"

"Good enough. Straight procedure. You're DEA?"

The man with the gun nodded.

"Figured. Oh, damn. I called David Wong from this phone. You're tracking all calls to him at the bank and at home, so you traced back and found the address. From there it was simple. What took you so long?"

The man shrugged, stood, took the .45 out of Hawke's waistband, and looked at the twelve-shot magazine.

"Damn, I've heard about these. You really get thirteen shots without reloading?"

"Count them."

"You know where Balboa Park is?"

"Yep."

"Ever been there?"

"Yes. Do I win the quiz show?"

"You might. Never heard your last name. If David Wong knows it he never told me. I've got a hunch you used to be known as Matt Hawke."

"Do I look like a dangerous bird?"

"That you do. I can check your prints in an hour. You want me to do that?"

"Not especially."

"I was transferred to Manhattan a month ago. I put in six months in San Diego. I was not a big fan of Captain Lewis. I liked Will Halston, your ex-partner. He's well and just got a promotion. I heard about what happened to Carzeda. The whole area is still buzzing about how you took down Ramon and shattered the drug scene along the Cal-Mex border. Hey, everyone in the DEA isn't hunting you."

"Including you?"

"Especially me. I took credit for that cutting house wipeout in Queens. Gene over there does what I tell him. Hell, I'm glad you're in town. You went to Houston then Miami and on to Colombia I hear."

"Could be. So why the big trackdown? Why not just let me do my thing?"

"Curious, mostly. You had combat in 'Nam, right?"

"Could be."

"I never quite made it. Hell, I ducked it. The art air freight—you found the horse with the pictures?"

"They used it as packing, to keep the pictures safe. The customs man never even looked inside the burlap packing pads."

"City boys found two bodies up in Van Cortlandt Park. A

witness said two men gunned them down, then stole the new
light blue Caddy they drove. Another shipment?''

"If you know already . . ."

"I don't. I'm making a lot of assumptions."

"A hundred pounds of horse melted down in the Hudson.
It came in from Canada through customs. Junk was packed
into the rear seat cushion. No springs."

The DEA man took Hawke's .45 and pushed it into the
box of weapons under the bed. Then he held out his hand.

"Frank Edward, Manhattan office. I'm with Group Forty-
one. This joker behind you is Gene Ping, my passport into
Chinatown. Relax, Gene, he's friendly." They all shook
hands.

Hawke sat down on the bed and snorted. "I don't see the
purpose of this meet."

"It's a see-me. I wanted to see if I could find you. I also
thought you might share what you know about the New
Control with us."

"Why not. First, you better put some protection on David
Wong. Somebody from New Control contacted him to set
me up to be wasted tonight at the Fourteenth Street subway
station."

"Can I use your phone?" Frank asked.

Hawke nodded. The DEA man got an outside line, spoke
quietly, gave an address, and hung up. "It's done. I've got a
man on him twenty-four hours."

"You want to know about New Control. The head man is
Dong Chu. An illegal from Hong Kong. He's been here four
or five years. Came in through the Canadian border sieve.
May have backing and support of one of the Hong Kong
triads. May be a tool of 14K. I'm sure you know who they
are.

"The Golden Dragon is the key, at least for meet and
greet and sales contacts on the heroin.

"I know one of their salespeople. She turned, told me

most of what I know about the group. But I'm afraid she's
been blown. I can't contact her.

"The twelve young girl suicides with their brains blown
out . . . they're all victims, druggers who bottomed out, got
picked out of the gutter and made beautiful, then forced to
play Russian roulette in a betting den. It's six-to-one odds,
but at least twelve have lost the game.

"Chu runs it all, drugs, prostitution, protection, and
loan-sharking. He's set up on computer and is highly so-
phisticated. A lot of his horse is brought in not by wholesalers but by Chu and his people. That's about it. I don't know
where the GHQ is."

"Christ, you've got more in two days than we have in six
months. We're really trying to crack this outfit. I hear
they're running seventy-five percent of the horse in all five
boroughs."

"I'll help all I can. Now you know all about them I do.
I've given you some new information. May I be excused?"

"When we've got all sorts of wanted notices on you from
San Diego and from Houston and Miami?" Gene asked
"All murder warrants?"

Hawke looked at him. "How long have you been with the
agency?"

"Six months out of the academy."

"Congratulations on lasting so long."

Frank chuckled. "Gene, Hawke has done more of our
work for us in the last two days than we'll do in a year. He
doesn't have our legal restraints. Would you have planted
plastic explosives in that Queens house after blasting six
men into corpses?"

"Well, no. It's not proper procedure."

"So true," Hawke said. "You do it your way, kid. I have
to do it my way."

"Gene, I'll tell you about Hawke's wife later. For right
now, just be glad we hit it lucky and learned some more

about the New Control. You can write the report and put it down as an undisclosed but always reliable informant.''

"You mean we just walk out of here? What about that box of weapons?''

"Gene, I'm surprised at you. How can the man work if we take away his tools?''

"But there's an illegal submachine gun in there with a highly illegal silencer on it, and—''

"Gene, shut up,'' Frank said. He turned back to Hawke. "You'll probably want to change your address. I won't bother you, for damned sure. But it would take the temptation away from Gene here. Might want to live in a car in an alley somewhere. Isn't too bad for a few nights.''

Frank stood and stretched. "It's damn nice to be right about a hunch.'' He shook Hawke's hand. "Hey, you need anything, give me a call.'' He handed Hawke his card. "On Group Forty-one I have a lot of latitude. Anything but buy-money. That they want tracked to a loss or a bust.''

"Thanks, nothing I need right now but information you don't have either.''

Frank grinned. "Stay out of trouble. Give me a call before you leave town if you have time. Hey, not all of us in the DEA are assholes.''

They all laughed and the two government men went out the door. Hawke let them get to the street, then he packed up, put all the weapons and grenades from the cardboard box into his partly filled suitcase, and checked out.

He walked a mile farther uptown and found a small hotel where he registered. Tomorrow he would rent another car.

Hawke looked out his hotel window at a small slice of Manhattan lights, windows, and walls. What happened to Lin Liu? He was afraid that he would never find out.

CHAPTER
EIGHT

Hawke watched the Manhattan night for a while, then called David Wong. David picked up the phone on the first ring.

"Wanted to let you know I checked out the lead and it was what you thought it was. The only message they had was death."

"Glad you got away."

"Also met your friend Frank Edwards. We had a chat. I told him all I know about the operation. He didn't arrest me. Nice guy."

"Good, now he won't bug me." David hesitated. "Don't know if I should tell you this or not, but I got what might be another lead. A guy came to the bank this afternoon and asked me if I was Shensi's brother. He said he had a daughter killed by the same people, and he was sure it wasn't suicide. We talked for half an hour at my desk.

"He seemed sincere. Said he found my name as a survivor in the newspaper. He sounded honest. But now I've been wondering. He told me he thought he knew where some of these New Control people worked. He gave me an address and said it was downstairs.''

"Maybe. Is it in Chinatown?"

"Right in the middle. Couldn't be more dangerous for you."

"Doesn't sound right, like a setup."

"That's why I didn't tell you before. But I wanted to talk to you about it. I'm glad you're working closer to the bastards. It still makes me so mad I can't think straight."

"We'll get some of them, David."

"Frank called again, maybe ten minutes ago. He said he had a real tip for you. One they had tried but didn't have enough evidence for a warrant. Said something about it was a collection point for pushers to pick up their goods."

"Frank knows I'll take it down if I can. What's the address? You want to come along in case I get lost?"

"What about Buzz?"

"He's at the show waiting for Jasmine. They really hit it off."

"Yes, I'd like to come. Maybe I can do a little more than just talk about these people."

"I don't have a car anymore. Can we take a taxi?"

"Sure." He gave Hawke the address. They agreed to meet on the corner across the street in half an hour.

Hawke opened his suitcase and looked at the tools of his trade. What would work best for this in-close situation? He took the Uzi, removed the silencer, and hung the subgun on a cord around his neck.

Into his belt he pushed the .45 with the silencer, and two spare twelve-round magazines went in his pocket. He wore the old army fatigues with the big pockets low on the thigh.

He put on the old army shirt and let it hang outside to cover the Uzi and its magazine with thirty rounds of .45. He was glad he had Frank's phone number if they needed it.

The taxi let him off at a corner a block down from the meeting place, and he walked along the Chinatown street.

Most of the small shops and restaurants were closed. He saw David on the corner in a pair of jeans and a wild plaid shirt.

Hawke came up behind him and touched his shoulder. Wong jumped two feet.

"Ready?" Hawke asked.

"Not really, but I know it's something I need to do. It's that herb store over there, the one with the two young men outside screening everyone before they get inside."

"Good to know. I'll go first, roust the pair with my .45, then you come up and we'll push them inside and take everyone in the shop with us into the back room." Hawke watched him. "You going to be okay? Nobody gets killed tonight."

Hawke walked away, meandering along, one hand under his shirt. He stared at a store next to the herb retailer, then moved that way, slowly. The two Red Stick guards out front watched him, then discounted him and looked at other people on the sidewalk.

As soon as the closest guard shifted his glance away, Hawke surged toward him, shoved the silenced .45 in his belly and pushed him backward to the store's front door.

The other guard looked over. He was only four feet away.

"Get in here with us, or your buddy has a lead dinner," Hawke growled. David Wong hurried up, bumped into the Red Stick, and shoved him toward the door.

Then they were inside. Hawke saw the back door less than twenty feet away down the center aisle. He pushed the Red Sticks that way, frisking the first one, taking a .38 from his belt. Hawke grabbed the other guard, picked a .45 from his shoulder and hustled them and the owner of the little store ahead of him into the back room.

There three older Chinese men sat around smoking.

"Up! Up! On your feet!" Hawke bellowed. "Everyone move out the back door. Now! Move or somebody dies!"

The men jumped up and hurried ahead of him. David

Wong brought up the rear, watching behind him. The next room was a small one, with a hall that led forward and then down steps. Hawke directed them to move that way.

At the bottom of the steps a guard watched, amused. Hawke put a silenced .45 slug into the wall beside him.

"You, with the grin! Down on your face on the floor. Now, or you're buzzard bait!" The young Chinese man fell to the floor at once.

The next door led into a large room with more than a dozen people in it. There was a counter where a man sat taking in money and marking an account book. His hand darted down and Hawke put two shots from the silenced autoloader past his head into the wall as a warning.

"Leave your hardware in place or you're dead!" Hawke barked at him. He looked around.

"Buddy, get the other door!" Hawke roared at Wong. He rushed through the people and blocked the far exit.

Hawke pulled the Uzi up from the cord around his neck and sent a burst of six unsilenced rounds into the far wall high up. A woman fainted. Then it was totally silent.

Hawke ran to the man with the books and pushed him to the floor. He kicked the man along the side of his head once and he fell unconscious.

"Everyone line up and come past me single file!" Hawke brayed at the people. "If you have any drugs, put them on the table. I find anybody holding out, I'll machine-gun you. Understand? Move!"

He frisked the men as they came by. Only one had a weapon. He pushed them into a row along the far wall and made them sit down and cross their arms and legs.

"Stay that way. We'll get along fine." He looked at the account books. "Wong, translate this for me."

David Wong scanned the books. "Christ . . . these are the accounts for each of these pushers. It shows about forty sellers working out of the place."

There were twenty men in the room.

"We'll wait for the rest," Hawke said. "Look around in those shelves and cupboards and see if you can find any cash stashed away."

David Wong searched the area and a closet and came out with two grocery-size paper sacks stuffed with rolls and bundles of bills. He put them on the table beside the account books.

"Use his shoelaces and belt, and tie up the distributor over there. Looks like he's coming back to consciousness."

Wong did as suggested. Three young Chinese men walked in and stared in surprise.

"Welcome to five to ten years in prison, gents," Hawke said, waving the Uzi at them. "Come right in and get frisked, then take your place in the lineup over there."

When the men had been checked and sat down, Hawke asked Wong to call Frank Edwards.

"You want him down here?"

"Right, it's his bust. Just tell him to come damn fast and bring some manpower and a bus to transport these people to the slammer."

They waited and welcomed each new pusher as he came in. There were six women now in the group.

Thirty minutes after Wong made the call, Edwards slipped in the door, his .38 leading the way.

"The party for tonight?" Edwards asked with a big grin.

"Tonight's the night, Frank. You got some help?"

"Yeah, but I figured you might want to slip out the back way first. You and Dave."

"Sure you can handle them? I could loan you a chopper," Hawke said, lifting the subgun.

Edwards laughed. "I've got six men right on the other side of that door. Get out of here."

Hawke picked up one of the sacks of money. "This is for expenses; the rest of the cash and all the horse is yours. I always try to repay friends who help me."

Frank gave Hawke a salute as he and David Wong went

through the far door, up some stairs, and into an alley. Hawke had the Uzi hidden under the floppy shirt again and carried the money sack like it was filled with cornflakes and tonight's dinner.

"How much money is in there?" Wong asked.

"I'll let you know when I count it."

They slid gently out of the alley and walked down toward a main drag where there were some taxis.

"How do you feel?" Hawke asked.

"Better, yeah, lots better. I finally helped smash some of the bastards who hurt Shensi."

"See anyone there who you know, or who knows you?"

He thought a moment. "No, I don't think so. But a lot of people see me in the bank who I never notice."

"Be better if you stayed in a hotel tonight. Just check in and check out in the morning."

"I'll see."

Hawke saw the car slam down the street, jump the curb, and come sweeping down the narrow sidewalk beside the solid front of the building. There was no place to hide on that side.

They both lunged into the street, away from the careening car. It slammed on the brakes, skidded past some garbage cans, and smashed a shop window. Two mean leapt from the car, handguns winking in the darkness like a pair of fireflies.

Hawke and Wong knelt behind a parked car. Hawke lifted the silenced .45 autoloader and fired twice. He came down and bobbed up over the hood and fired three times. One of the men sighed and slid to the pavement, a large hole where his right eye had been.

The second man ran forward screaming. Hawke waited for him to get closer. When the attacker came within six steps of the sedan that protected him, Hawke lifted up and fired three times, as fast as he could pull the silenced autoloader's trigger.

Two of the slugs caught the charging Chinese man in the

chest; the last one punched through the top of his forehead and exited with a half cup of brains, skull, and vital nerve centers. He slammed into the car, rolled off the fender, and littered the street with his body.

Hawke grabbed David Wong and they sprinted up the street. A NYPD patrol car's siren wailed as it turned into the narrow way.

David pointed into a doorway, pushed through and into a small room that had once been a shop but now was a residence.

David called out softly in Chinese, and an elderly man came to an open doorway. David chattered with him quickly in their native language, then the man nodded.

"He understands our problem. He'll be glad to cover for us and get us through to the next alley. Come on!"

They ran through the house, into the alley, and then down through three more alleys, crossing streets to put some distance between them and the death scene.

All the time, Hawke had clutched the paper sack of money in one arm. He knew at least one stack of bills had fallen, but he wasn't going back to look for it.

He took two packets of bills that he saw were hundreds and pushed them into David's hands.

"For your services as guide tonight," Hawke said.

David riffled the bills like the banker he was. "Goddamn! They're all hundreds ... must be eight to ten thousand here."

"Enjoy," David said. "Help pay Jasmine's rent."

He stepped into the street and flagged a taxi. It kept on going. Down a block they came to a brighter street, and Hawke got a cab. "I'll give you a call tomorrow," Hawke said. He eased into the seat and relaxed. For a moment he forgot what street his hotel was on. Then he remembered. He gave the address and settled back.

It had been a good night's work. The DEA would get

credit for a big bust, and New Control would wonder how in the hell the place had been busted. Good.

Later that night Hawke lay on his bed looking up at the regularly changing pattern of lights on the ceiling. A spotlight shining on a roof half a block over jolted through his window and outlined a shadow of the window on the far wall.

He was tired. Tired of the killing.

Did there have to be so much killing?

Absolutely! The drugger bastards must die.

He watched the flickering shadows on his ceiling of some moving sign outside somewhere. They all had to die, the way his wife had died. They were all unthinking, self-centered bastards who would sell their daughters for a fix.

They had to die.

Matthew J. Hawke did not start out in life to be Investigator-Judge-Executioner of the participants in the drug traffic.

He was born in Idaho, went to San Diego with his parents when he was six, and finished school there. Then he surged into the Vietnam conflict, learning weapons, understanding the kill-or-be-killed philosophy when most kids his age were still in high school or learning about college. He had killed a man before his eighteenth birthday.

He went on to become a top combat sergeant, with that certain touch that only the natural warrior knows. He was simply extremely good at the art of warfare and infiltration and combat—he was an expert killer. When he came back to San Diego he enrolled in the police academy just after his twenty-first birthday.

He was a SDPD cop for three years, working up to the narco squad and becoming expert in the narcotics problems of San Diego and Tijuana. The Drug Enforcement Administration approached him, explaining their larger job and wider scope. He joined.

For six years he battled drug dealers, smugglers, and infiltrators along the southern U.S. border. Then that fateful day in San Diego came and jolted him into a grief that he would never overcome. An eternal sadness.

It hadn't been that big a case; a wholesale dealer was bringing in a supply for a big dealer. Twenty pounds of cocaine. He and his partner had been on the smuggler's tail for two months, and now it was happening.

For three days Hawke had been playing the part of a street wino watching a fifth floor window in a deserted warehouse. Then it went down. The signal came. Hawke told his partner, using a "wire" radio on his chest, and charged into the building.

He found them on the fifth floor. Three of them, laughing, drinking, telling jokes. Twenty pounds of coke sat in one corner, half the room was spattered with blood. A mutilated, slashed, violated, broken, and naked body lay on a red-drenched table.

He killed two of them as he charged into the room. The other one, a Colombian, said the torture wasn't his doing. Hawke had kept his big .45 trained on the man as he checked the body to see if it was still alive. It had been a woman! Both breasts had been cut off. Her arms broken in several places, her ankles and legs broken, her fingernails pulled out, then her fingers sliced off. A broom handle extended from her crotch. Every inch of her body had been slashed and slashed again with sharp knives or razors so she would bleed an unending red river onto the table.

The Mafia called it making "turkey meat." The victim was tortured for hours, for days, for as long as possible and still kept alive, to make her suffer as much as was humanly possible. In the end she died from loss of blood.

"Bastards!" Hawke shouted, remembering that traumatic, that shattering day.

Her long blond hair had been cut off and left on the desk, the stubble burned down to her scalp. The woman had been brutalized to the greatest extent that a human being can be.

Then he saw the untouched, perfect face and he discovered

the woman was his wife, Connie. He hadn't seen her for three days, not since he started this stakeout. He shook in a rage so devastating that he had no way to vent it, to avenge such a terrible, such a pain-saturated death. Hawke let the wracking sobs come. They tore through him as though he were a shaft of sunlight being shattered by a shadow, smashing him against the walls, shredding him in the hurricane winds, plunging him into a raging maelstrom of hatred.

He had killed the Colombian slowly, shooting him in the thigh when he tried to run. He let the man suffer a moment, then shot him in the right knee, then in the left knee.

The Colombian drug producer fainted. When he came back to consciousness and when he suffered again, Hawke shot him twice in his genitals.

When the Colombian could look up, Matthew J. Hawke, the man the San Diego papers soon called The Avenger, shot the drugger in the forehead.

Then he left the room, quit the DEA, and launched his own private war on drugs, drug sellers, importers, and producers.

Now he shifted his position on the bed, sat up, and looked out the Manhattan window.

No, it was not time yet for the war to end. There were many battles to be fought. There were thousands of enemies out there. Men and women who tried to seduce the nation on drugs, to hook them, to trap them into selling their minds and their bodies into a short, hard life of addiction.

While he had a breath left he would fight them. Yes, he would probably be killed one of these days. He had gone into the fight that first time in San Diego not really caring if he lived or died. After he had wiped out Ramon he would be ready to die if he had to.

He had survived and continued in a fight against drugs wherever he found them. He would do so until the day he finally died.

Lin Liu might be another one who had been lost to the ravages of drugs. But if she had, it was after she had won her personal fight and had begun to strike back at them.

If they had caught her somehow, he prayed that her death would be quick and easy. He wasn't sure his sanity could survive another turkey meat corpse.

Hawke lay down, and far, far into the night, he finally slept.

Mister Chu had spoken privately with all twenty of his top people in his master control room. The vicious traitor had to be one of these twenty. No one else in his organization knew what was needed to cause all the hell that had hit the New Control in the last two days. Two shipments lost, a cutting room smashed, and now one of his prime wholesalers knocked out by the DEA.

How could anyone outside of his closely welded group know of all these plans?

A traitor!

He would find the one. He had three prime suspects. Two men and a woman. All now sat in bare rooms with their sins on their minds. All would be questioned again.

All were naked in a room without any furniture.

One of them would crack.

Already Lin Liu had told him that she had talked with the white man, and they had made a try for him at the hotel.

"Damn him to hell!" Mister Chu roared. The tough American had killed two of his princesses. But did Lin Liu know about the cutting room and the two shipments? Not necessarily. She had confessed that she desired the man and had made love to him in his hotel and had not reported it, but such a small infraction did not mean that she was the real culprit.

Had the American, known only as Matt, been responsible for part of the problem? He knew the DEA Group Forty-one had been in on two of the raids. The shipments were the most costly. Who had told about them?

He called in his most trusted right arm, Yen Kao.

Yen stood stiffly at attention in front of his leader. He had been a street tough until Mister Chu had picked him up, trained him and let him grow to the top of the organization. He would always be thankful.

"Yes, Mister Chu. How may I help you?"

"Can we change the arrival of the shipment tomorrow?"

"We have no communication with the small plane for security purposes. I'm afraid it is impossible. We can double or triple the number of men and guns meeting the shipment."

"Yes, do so. Keep the area sealed off from every road-way. If anyone tries to get in, detain or kill them."

"It shall be done."

"Who is hurting us, Kao? You know our people as well as I do. You know who I have in custody."

"Not the girl. Lin Liu treats you as a messiah. You found her dead and gave her back life. She would never betray you."

"She did sleep with the white man."

"She is a woman, and weak in certain ways. But she is strong and loyal. I admit I am swayed. For a year I have wanted her."

"When this is over, she is yours, Kao. You should have told me. Bring in Toy."

Kao left at once, went to the detention room, and tied the male prisoner's hands behind his back and marched him naked through the nearly empty offices and into a special interrogation room next to the end.

Three women workers were in the room as well as three other men, Kao, and Mister Chu. Merely being naked among those dressed is a powerful force working against the prisoner. The man suspect, Ken Toy, would not look at any of those in the room.

"Toy!" Mister Chu snapped.

The accused looked up. Mister Chu stood on a platform so he glared down on the man. Bright lights shone into Toy's face.

"You knew of the three shipments to arrive this week?"

"Yes sir."

"Why?"

"I helped set up the type of travel, the route, and assigned men to either bring in the goods or to meet them."

"You told someone about the shipments, didn't you, Toy?"

"No, Mister Chu. I am loyal to you and to the New Control. You brought me into your organization when I had nothing. I will be forever thankful to you. I would do nothing to harm you or the cause."

"You lie!" Mister Chu jumped down near Toy and hit him with a spiked three-inch-wide board. The razor-sharp spike sank into Toy's chest an inch deep, then the board slapped him backward a step. Mister Chu pulled the board away from his chest and watched a line of blood run down his belly, not stopping until it came to his pubic hair.

"You told someone about the shipments!"

"My master, with all due respect, I told no one."

"Kill him!" Mister Chu screamed.

Yen Kao stepped forward with a small pistol and aimed it at Toy's head. He turned toward Mister Chu. "If I kill him now, we will not know for sure if he's the traitor or not."

Mister Chu walked around in a circle slowly, his hands clasped behind his back. At last he looked up. "Yen, you are right. You are almost always right. Take him back to his room. Bring in the woman."

Lin Liu heard them coming. She stood by the wall facing the door, her head high. There was nothing they could do to her without killing her that she had not experienced before. Nothing. She had no fear. Yet her chin quivered as the door opened, and one of the guards motioned her forward.

She walked quickly, making them walk faster to keep up. At the door she let them open it, then walked in, as naked as Toy had been. One of the women in the room looked away. Mister Chu saw it and sent the witness out of the room.

"Traitor," Mister Chu said softly.

"No, Mister Chu. How can I be a traitor when I am already dead three times? Three times I put the silver revolver to my head and pulled the trigger. Three times I died, only to live again.

"Then you said I was forever finished with the game. How can I be a traitor to you who has killed me three times already?"

"What? you talk in riddles."

"All of life is a riddle, Mister Chu. I used to wonder what life was about when I lay in the gutter begging for a fix. Why are people, Mr. Chu? Have you ever asked yourself that? Why is a species called man roaming this planet? The planet Earth would be so much better off without man. Then the forests would flourish, the birds and the animals would prosper and multiply, and the biggest animal, man, would not slaughter them."

Mister Chu screamed at her and slapped her, spinning her whole body around and jolting her into one of the Red Sticks near her.

"Shut up! Shut up! Shut up! You sound like my old schoolmaster. You know what happened to him? I killed him before I left Hong Kong and jammed his fingers into his mouth!"

"Then he could never yell at you again, could he," Lin said. She wasn't sure why she was being so glib, so calm, so casual with Mister Chu. Before she had been afraid of him. Now she wasn't. He couldn't hurt her now. She had already died three times.

Mister Chu slapped her again, almost knocking her down.

A large welt showed on her cheek. Lin nearly fell but caught her balance.

"Did you tell the white man about the shipments?" Mister Chu asked her. He stood directly in front of her now, started to reach out to fondle her breasts but stopped.

Lin stared at him. She lied without flinching, with a flicker of her eyes, without a nerve jumping.

"No," she said.

"Take her away! They're both lying. I'll punish all three. By the time I've pulled out three fingernails from each of them, I'll know which one is the bastard of a traitor!"

Mister Chu stormed out of the room. Yen Kao touched Lin's shoulder and nodded, and he walked with her to her detention cell. She had always been a favorite of his. He frowned when he saw her swollen cheek.

"I'll do what I can for you," he said. "It might not be enough. I've never seen him like this."

"He's never been so close to losing before," Lin said and walked into the room. She wondered if she would get out of it alive.

CHAPTER
NINE

Before the dew had dried the next morning, Hawke had rented a car using his last set of ID and paying five hundred in advance. The clerk said they seldom got that kind of advance, but Hawke told her he always did it that way.

By nine o'clock he had called Buzz and set up the meeting at the chopper pad on the Hudson River.

"The bird from the west should be flying in about eleven-thirty, plenty of time."

Hawke stayed at the car and gave money to Buzz to put a thousand-dollar deposit on the chopper rental. The clerk said since Buzz was a repeat customer, they didn't need to keep his pilot's license. Instead he took a fake ID of Hawke's that Buzz carried and copied it down, and they took off.

Closter, New Jersey, was their target. It's a village north of New York across from Yonkers. It has a small landing field and a tower with radio control, but not a lot of traffic. More of a weekender spot for New York sports to fly their vintage planes from and to take flying lessons. It's not far east of the Hudson River.

They arrived there early. Buzz contacted the tower and asked permission to land in the chopper area. Said he had some local business. He was given landing instructions, and when he came down he left the radio on, set to the tower frequency.

"With the radio we can know when the New Control's bird will be coming. We'll also find out where it's going to land."

Buzz handed Hawke a copy of the *Times*. A front page story and picture showed more than thirty Chinese men being marched on board a bus outside a Chinese herb store.

"You playing games last night without my help?"

"David Wong had a tip from the DEA man. We took down the place, then called his DEA contact and he took over. Nobody even got shot up there last night."

"You slipping?"

"Didn't want to shock David too much. You watched Jasmine's show last night?"

"Yeah, and it's great! Even the third time. Jasmine is perfect. We seem to hit it off just about right."

"Sounds serious."

"It could be—but I've only known her a few days."

"Sometimes it doesn't take long."

The radio crackled with landing instructions, but it was a bigger plane.

Hawke took out his suitcase and let Buzz select the weapon he wanted. He grabbed the Beretta 93-R. Hawke slung the Uzi around his neck on the cord and took off the silencer. He screwed the hush tube on his .45 and pushed it into his belt.

He wore chinos today and a sport shirt that wasn't big enough to hide the Uzi. But today there would be no need for hiding. He picked up one of the WP hand grenades and pushed it in his big pocket. "Might come in handy," he said. "We might not have enough time to load up the heroin. We'll take alternate action."

A half hour later they heard tower talk that interested them.

"Closter, this is Piper Comanche 467 over the Hudson requesting landing instructions."

"Yes, 467, we have you. Use the north-south. Continue on your present course until you clear the park, then start your normal landing pattern. We have a ten MPH west wind, visibility unlimited."

"Thank you Closter. Just leaving the park and starting the down-leg."

"Roger, 467, proceed."

"Sounds like it could be our pigeon," Buzz said.

They watched a silver and blue Piper Comanche come in on the north-south runway. When it was down the radio chattered again.

"Tower, this is 467. Request outlying parking spot for transfer of highly volatile oxygen bottles for lung patients. We'll be met by an ambulance."

"Roger, 467. Taxi to the far end of your present runway and take the apron to the left. Park near the airport fence."

"Roger, tower."

"Up and at 'em," Buzz said. He started the chopper and let it warm up for the required sixty seconds. It was still warm.

"Ambulance just left the parking area heading for the end of that taxi strip," Hawke grated. "Must be the New Control pickup team. They would ask for the action to be well away from any witnesses."

They lifted off and hedgehopped toward the Comanche, which had stopped near the fence and had cut power. The ambulance rolled toward the spot.

"Chopper 161, you're operating in a hazardous manner," the tower radio blared.

Buzz shut off the radio.

The ambulance came closer to the Comanche. It would beat them there. Hawke watched as the small plane's side door opened and the pilot and another man stood there with several large, plastic wrapped packages waiting for the ambulance.

"Looks like our meat," Hawke said. "Damn sure not oxygen cylinders."

They slammed over the ambulance at twenty feet just as it stopped beside the plane. One of the aircraft's men pulled a pistol out of his belt and waved it at them.

"Unfriendly natives," Buzz said. "Just like in 'Nam."

"Let's give them one more chance," Hawke said. He lifted the side door and charged a round into the subgun. They came in from upwind. Just as they flew within pistol range, one of the men stopped tossing plastic wrapped packages, lifted a .45, and blasted three rounds.

All shots missed, but it was the ID Hawke needed. He leveled in the Uzi sideways and chattered a dozen rounds into the unloading operation. One man went down with a slammer through the side of his head. Another dove for cover.

Hawke turned the chopper on the ambulance and riddled the radiator and front tires as they slashed past the drug transfer. Buzz swept around in a climbing turn and came back at ground level, with the skids not three feet off the ground.

A rifle poked out the door of the ambulance, but Hawke saw it and sent ten rounds through the door, chopping the gunner into a bloody corpse.

"Set it down," Hawke barked.

The chopper came to earth fifty feet from the ambulance. Hawke hit the ground running, the Uzi up and ready. One man stepped out from the ambulance with an Ingram and blasted a dozen rounds at Hawke, but the range was too great and they dispersed over a twenty-foot area.

Hawke lifted the longer-ranged Uzi with its higher power

and cut the man in half. He darted to the left, around the silent ambulance, and paused. He heard someone groaning in the plane. Buzz had worked up on the other side. Hawke cleared the ambulance. Two corpses, nobody in back.

He stepped cautiously toward the Comanche. A Chinese man leaped out of the plane with pistols in both hands, firing furiously. Before Hawke could bring up the Uzi, a three-round burst came from behind the gunner and he screamed, dove forward, and died on the tarmac.

Buzz came under the plane. "That's the ball game. Lots of horse, not much else."

A pair of sirens wailed from across the airport a half mile away.

"Company. I'll check the ambulance." Inside the blood-splashed vehicle of mercy, Hawke found what he hoped he might: a suitcase bulging with cash. He carried it out and gauged the speed of the police cars heading their way.

"Let's leave it for the feds." He waved the grenade at Buzz, who ran for the chopper. Hawke pulled the pin and tossed the WP grenade in the back of the small plane, then he ran.

Then, 4.2 seconds later, the white phosphorus grenade went off, spraying burning phosphorus throughout the plane and into the ambulance. Nothing can put out burning phosphorus. It's a true incendiary. The inside of the plane caught fire at once, and the flames crept toward the ambulance.

Hawke ran for the chopper, tossed in the suitcase of money, jumped in himself, and shut the door just as Buzz lifted off and darted forward, away from the two police cars now less than a hundred yards distant and away from six more dark red sedans that raced across the airport behind the official cars.

Just before the cars reached the burning aircraft, the fuel tanks on the plane or the ambulance exploded, drenching both rigs in flaming gasoline.

The chopper kept to treetop height as it traveled due north

over the New Jersey countryside toward the state line with New York. Once the helicopter was out of sight of the airport, Buzz turned it back across the Hudson River.

Hawke patted the suitcase. "Double duty. We got the payoff money, and we dumped the goods. Heroin won't burn, but the fire sure will leave a dirty pile of white powder for the police and firemen to inspect."

"Those red sedans," Buzz said. "Suppose those were from your friends in the New Control?"

"Wouldn't be at all surprised. Where we going to set this rig down?"

"We can't go back to the heliport. Either those cops back there or the tower have our ID number for damn sure. How about in a park up here somewhere? Then we dodge cops and grab a taxi."

That's the way it went down. Buzz landed in Tibbets Brook Park in Yonkers, down near McLean Avenue. They took the suitcase of weapons and the second one of money and walked through the park for half a mile before they hailed a taxi.

They changed cabs three times before they wound up back at the heliport. Hawke slipped inside the parking area and drove out without attracting any attention. He picked up Buzz, who had arrived by taxi that morning.

"Go ahead," Hawke said, laughing. "Look at the cash. Give me an estimate of how much is there."

Buzz unstrapped the suitcase and opened it.

"Jesus! Look at that! I deal with big sums of money sometimes but it's just a number on a check. This is the real stuff!"

"How much is there?" Hawke asked.

"If horse is still going for sixty thousand a pound and we messed up one hundred pounds, that should be six million dollars!"

"Close enough," Hawke said. The Avenger watched Buzz. "You ready to go back to work?"

"Hell no! I'm ready to sign up for another tour of 'Nam! We got a war anywhere these days where a hot chopper pilot can report for a little wild action? Christ, but these last three days have been a kick in the old ass. I'd forgotten how mashed potatoes and rice I've become in the last ten years.

"I'm in one gigantic rut. No thrills, no excitement . . . no fucking danger!"

"True, but you're not twenty-one years old any more, either. Then there's Jasmine to consider."

Buzz snorted and looked out the window. "You slam a guy back to reality in a rush, don't you, Hawke?"

"You're a part-time soldier, Buzz. Next week you'll be holding little old ladies' hands when their stock drops a quarter. You'll be taking rich guys to lunch; you'll be grabbing at rumors and hoping they're not insider information. With me it's different. I signed up for the duration."

Buzz slouched in the seat. "Yeah, yeah, I know. But it's such a damned high! I tried marijuana once—that high was nowhere near what these past few days have been."

"Your life wasn't on the line before. Nobody was shooting at you. It's always a gut thrill when you go out in a kill or be killed situation. But it's also no way for most men to live. Especially if you want to last long enough to play with your grandchildren."

"Oh, damn! I had a date for lunch today with Jasmine."

"You're late."

"Drop me off at the next phone you see. Maybe I can salvage something." He grinned. "Oh, you'll probably want this back." He handed Hawke the Beretta.

A half hour later, Hawke called David Wong. The bank operator said David hadn't been in to work that morning. He didn't call in. Hawke swore and dug into his wallet and came up with Frank Edward's DEA card and his phone number.

He got right through. "Frank, you heard from David this morning?"

"No. Anything wrong?"

"He didn't go to work. Could you check out his place?"

"Good idea. I'm not far from there. I'm on a cellular from my car. I'm still up to my elbows writing up charges. First time we've ever busted that many pushers at once. All we can charge them with is possession, but it's a good start. We've been wanting to bust that supplier for a year."

"I'll call you back on this number in an hour to find out what you learn at David's."

Hawke stopped at a small restaurant, bought a sandwich and two cups of coffee. It was his first meal of the day. Then he called Frank. The agent came on sounding tired and angry.

"No answer at his place. I went inside and the apartment was a mess. There had been a fight there. I found some blood, but it could have been a bloody nose. So far I'm not saying anything to anyone about this."

"No cops there?"

"No. I want to let it cool off a bit."

"I'm going over and check it out," Hawke said. "I got him into this; I have to try to get him out of it."

"This number is good twenty-four hours. I take this cellular to bed with me and to the john. Call me if you need anything."

When Hawke pulled up three doors down from David Wong's four story apartment house, he saw nothing unusual. He had been there before.

Hawke watched the apartment house for half an hour. He still saw nothing to alarm him. There were no lookouts that he could see watching those who went in or came out. Nobody idling away who shouldn't be on the street. No red sedan lurking a few doors down with all the windows rolled up.

He left his car, pulled the floppy hat well down over his face, and put on the reflectorized sunglasses. Two minutes later he was at David's apartment. He picked the lock and went in.

The room was a mess. Furniture tipped over, a trail of drops of blood out of the kitchen. Hawke looked at the telephone. It remained on the hook. Near it was a notepad, but no convenient name and number were listed. A magazine lay nearby with ink marks on it. As he looked at it harder, he realized the *O*s in the headlines had been filled in with a pen.

A doodle. He looked at the magazine cover again. Down in the picture was some writing. He turned it to the light and could make out the blue writing on the dark print of the picture. A phone number. He copied it on the scratch pad thinking that it looked familiar.

One glance at Frank's DEA card from his pocket showed him why he thought he knew the number. It was the same as that for Frank Edwards, except for the last two digits. Many companies give direct dialing to people that way. The call could have been from somebody in the DEA office.

Hawk dialed it. A woman came on the line. "This is Gene Ping's phone; I'm picking up for him. Any message?"

Hawke hung up.

Ping, Edward's DEA partner. What the hell was going on? Had Ping called yesterday to tell David that Frank wanted to see him? Possible. Or he could have called to tell David to stay home for a meeting—and sent in a pair of assassins.

Ping was Chinese. So, the pope is Catholic, the rabbi is Jewish. Still . . .

Hawke eased out of the apartment, walked through the back door and down the alley. In the next street he found a pay phone and dialed Frank's number. He came on the first ring.

"Yeah?"

"Frank, this is Matt. How tight are you with Gene Ping?"

"Been with me a month. Just a kid learning. Doing a good job. Has some know-how of Chinatown, which helps."

"Did you ask him to call David Wong last couple of days?"

"Hell no, I make my own calls."

"So why was Ping's number handwritten on that magazine near David's phone?"

"You found that?"

"Just now." He rattled off the number.

"Shit!"

"Why?"

"We've had a leak around Forty-one. Not sure who or how."

"Could be. My guess is David Wong has been snuffed."

"Damn! That will hang heavy around my neck for a long time if that's true." There was some dead air.

"Look, this is a land line, so no airwaves on the cellular. I'm in the office. No leaks. I'll set up a meet with you and Gene."

"Frank, tell him I need to have some Chinese hood ID'd. He can help me but you can't, something like that. We meet at Pell and Johnson. If Gene can ID this guy for me, it could lead to a good-size bust and maybe a cutting room."

"Better yet, Matt, leave me out of it, so I don't know. Say you tried to get me and then asked for his number, or I gave it to you before." He paused. "Oh, word out in Chinatown is that your head, preferably in a bucket, is worth a cool million dollars. Gene might even go for that as a bonus. Cover your back down there."

"Will do. I just called and Ping was out. When will he come in?"

Edwards let the line go dead for a minute. "He just came in. I'll check out with him, then you give it five minutes and call him. Oh, hey, buddy, good luck!"

"I'll need it."

Five minutes later Hawke used the same phone and called Gene Ping. He answered on the second ring.

"Gene? This is Matt. I couldn't get Frank and I've got a rush problem. I'm supposed to be meeting a guy down in Chinatown this afternoon. He says he's clean, no ties to nobody, but I sure would appreciate it if you could be there and ID him for me and give me a nod if he's clean. I don't want to walk into a trap down there."

"Sounds like a good, reasonable way to work. You have a time?"

"Let's see, it's just after three now. He said he'd be there at four. Would that give you enough time?"

"Plenty. You talked to Frank today?"

"Missed him twice on the phone. He must be tied up on something."

"He is, busy all day. Hey, Matt, I can handle this for you. I know a lot of the lowlife down there. If this guy is a knife man or out to rip you off, we'll nail him together."

"Great. Oh, he said meet him on the corner of Pell and Johnson—you know where that is?"

"Johnson, yeah, about three blocks up from Mott Street."

"Got it. I'll be wearing chinos and a sport shirt and an old army hat. See you at four."

Hawke hung up and went back to his car. Plenty of time. He took a hand grenade from his suitcase of arms and put it in his pocket. The .45 without the silencer made a bulge under his shirt. He pulled a larger, fuller shirt from his suitcase and put it on. Was this what they meant by living out of a suitcase?

Hawke took a roll of bills out of the latest haul of drug payoff money and stuffed it in his pocket. Then he put both suitcases in the Mustang's trunk and made sure it was locked.

He was ready. Either Gene Ping was a leak in the DEA and working for Mister Chu, or he was clean. In an hour he would know. Of course, Matthew J. Hawke might also be dead in an hour, but at least he would know about Ping. The grenade would be the key. Most civilians were scared shitless of a hand grenade.

Most people don't know how they work, how they are armed, and what makes them go off. A fragger was always good shock value and a great bluff weapon if he needed it.

He drove to the edge of Chinatown, parked his rental three doors from a NYPD precinct station, and walked down to Pell past Mott and stopped a block from Johnson. He found a cafe and ordered a cup of coffee and a donut.

It was a judgment call, but the more he remembered Gene Ping, the more he decided that Ping was the leak in the DEA and a loyal worker for Mister Chu. Big money can turn almost anyone if the benefits are great enough. He wondered how much Ping was getting paid a week in cash to be a traitor to the DEA.

Hawke watched the sidewalk on all four corners of the intersection. He had not designated one. At five minutes to four he saw Gene Ping arrive. He got out of a taxi and looked at each corner, then stood on the one where he had arrived. At once he started a rotating search of the corners watching for someone.

Hawke saw no sign, no indication that there were others there waiting for him to finger the man who needed to be killed. That could be the only reason for Ping to set him up: A million dollars tax free is still quite a bit of money, even with inflation.

Hawke let Ping stew for ten more minutes. He had critically dissected each of the four corners, but found no lurking danger. It was there, probably just inside a shop somewhere. He guessed there would be eight of them. Now he wished he had put the silencer on the .45. The damn Uzi would have been more intimidating.

He felt the indentations on the hand grenade shell in his pocket as he walked up to Ping and tapped his shoulder.

The tall, slender Chinese turned around and greeted him.

"Yeah, Matt. Been watching for you. Right now I don't see anyone who might be meeting you who is obviously dirty. Which corner was it supposed to be on?"

"Across the street," Hawke said, making a quick survey of the one he stood on, then across where the nearest shop door was, down about twenty feet.

"You're late," Ping said.

"Checking out the situation and the terrain. Were you ever in the service, Ping?"

"No, thank God."

"Too bad, teaches a man how to face death, how to rise above such a constant threat. Like now. There could be some muggers along here out for my scalp. I don't imagine Mister Chu likes me at all about now."

In spite of himself, Ping looked over sharply when he used the leader's name.

"Yeah, Ping, I know about Chu, and you know that I know. Isn't it proper to pronounce his name in public?"

"Not down here. This is the front lines."

They stepped up on the curb and Hawke kept looking around. "The little son-of-a-bitch said he would be here."

"So we wait for a while," Ping said.

Hawke saw three men come out of the nearest shop and look the other way. Across the street three more left a store there and waited for the light to change. They were coming.

"Oh, I need some cough drops," Ping said smoothly. "You mind if I duck into this place and get some?"

Hawke grabbed Ping by his belt in back, gripping the cinch tightly.

"You move more than three inches and you're a dead man, Ping."

"What 'en hell?"

"You know what. Don't signal them again. The three are still coming across the street and there are three more behind us looking the other way. Probably three or four more around."

Hawke checked behind him.

"We're backing up, just you and me, over to that brick wall. You get the picture, Ping?"

"No. What the hell are you talking about?"

"Keep your hands at your sides, Ping!" Hawke whispered in his ear with a sound of thunder behind it. "My .45 is on your spine. One slug might not kill you, but you'd be paralyzed from the neck down for life. That sound interesting? Let the Red Sticks start it."

The six men converged on them as they stood by the wall. Three more hurried up from the other direction. They stood as if waiting for a bus. Half of them turned each way.

"In English, Ping. Tell them to bug off or half of them are dead along with you. Mister Chu would not be pleased about that."

Ping said nothing.

Hawke had pulled the grenade from his pocket. He held it in his big hand, shielding it from the others, and pushed it up so Ping could see it, then pressed it against Ping's throat.

"Tell them, now!"

Ping cleared his throat. "Beat it, guys. Wrong man. Go on, get lost. He didn't show."

One or two of the Red Sticks scowled. One advanced at step.

Hawke turned his hand over and showed the grenade to the Chinese youth.

"Eager to die, asshole?" Hawke asked just loud enough so the kid could hear but no one else.

All nine of them turned and stared at the grenade. Hawke pulled the .45 and now put it around the other side of Ping, so the DEA agent-traitor was between his arms, shielding him.

"I'll get all nine of you. This is a thirteen-shot .45 in case you hadn't noticed. Now, who is going to be the first one to die?"

"Do what he says, get out of here!" Ping shouted. A

dozen people along the street turned to look. By then Hawke's grenade and the pistol were both out of sight.

"I'm counting to three, then you bastards start to die!" Hawke snarled. "You get the picture now? One." He paused. Two of the Red Sticks walked away. "Two," Hawke said. Five of them left quickly. Two faced him.

"Three!" Hawke spat. One turned and ran, the last one lunged forward. Hawke pushed the .45 into the Red Stick's soft belly and pulled the trigger once. The muffled report of the heavy weapon was almost swallowed up by the traffic noise.

The Red Stick staggered forward a step, then turned and fell. Hawke spun away. By now he had the grenade back in his pocket and his firm grip on Ping's belt in the back. He propelled Ping down the street away from the direction the Red Sticks had retreated.

"You did fair back there, Ping. That means you get to live just a few minutes longer." Fifty feet down, an alley cut through to the next block. It was jammed with small trucks, children playing, and a dozen resident street people.

Hawke pushed Ping up against a building halfway through and slammed the .45 down across his face. It was not meant to be kind; it was a punishing, tearing kind of blow. A section of Ping's cheek peeled down and the agent screamed.

Hawke punched him in the belly to relieve him of the excess air in his lungs, which cut off the scream.

"Now, Gene Ping. You and I are going to have a small talk. How much a week is Mister Chu paying you?"

He didn't answer.

Hawke slammed the side of his right hand into Ping's left kidney, then held him up as he started to go down. Ping vomited and his knees buckled, but Hawke kept him pinned to the wall.

"How much a week is Mister Chu paying you to spy on the DEA?"

The words came softly, hard to understand, but they were clear. "Five thousand."

"You're the reason the DEA hasn't been doing so well against Chinatown druggers?"

"Yes."

"Would you have shared the bonus for the million dollars on my head with the Red Sticks if they'd killed me?"

"No."

"Figures. Did you get extra for fingering David Wong for the assassins?"

"Didn't do that."

Hawke hit him in the other kidney and this time Ping had nothing left to vomit. When he could talk again, his pain-filled voice was little more than a whisper.

"All right. I took them there. I got twenty thousand extra."

"You'll never enjoy the money, Ping. You know that by now, don't you? Does Mister Chu suspect Lin Liu of helping me?"

"Yes, he suspects her."

"Where is his headquarters?"

"Kill me, but I'll never tell that."

"It might depend how slow I kill you, Ping."

"Won't matter."

"Ever had your fingernails pulled off with pliers, Ping?"

He shook his head; his eyes were vacant now, almost resigned. Without warning he lunged ahead, grabbed for Hawke's .45. He missed, crashed into Hawke, and both of them staggered backward.

Hawke brought up the .45, pushed it against Ping's side, and fired. The round took a slightly upward angle, missed most of his lungs, slashed through the top of his heart and tore up four major abdominal arteries. Ping was dead before Hawke let go of him, and he slid to the ground.

Hawke turned and walked away down the alley.

An eye for an eye. Ping for David Wong. He wasn't

positive David was dead, but with Mister Chu there was not much room for negotiating.

He walked around two blocks to the point where he had left his car and got in and drove. A dozen blocks later he saw a phone and stopped.

He phoned Frank Edwards.

"Yes. Edwards."

"Ping was the leak," Hawke said and hung up. He left the phone booth at once and drove back to his hotel. Hawke parked as close as he could, then carried both of his bags up to his room and fell on the bed.

Lin Liu was under suspicion. With Mister Chu that would mean interrogation, being locked in a room, and torture.

"Dammit, where in hell is Mister Chu's headquarters?"

CHAPTER

TEN

Jasmine Wong walked along Broadway thinking what a beautiful day it was, how great it was to be alive, and how lucky she was. The sun was out, she had a serious boyfriend for the first time in more than a year, and she was dancing almost every night in a show on Broadway. What more could a girl ask?

At the next cross street a car blocked the way, trapped in the crowds crossing the street. Two young men of her race shrugged and grinned. She smiled back at them. She was out on a mission of pleasure, to buy a new dress to wear on her date with Buzz tonight. Oh, what a sweetheart he was!

When she started to cross the next side street, she saw a car double-parked and extending halfway into the crosswalk. Some people were unkind and thoughtless. They shouldn't do that. She shrugged it off and started around the car.

Two young men jumped away from the curb, grabbed her, and before she could shout, one clamped his hand over her mouth and they lifted her into the back seat of the double-parked car. As the light changed it jolted forward and charged across Broadway.

The hand came away from her mouth and she screamed.

"I told you she would scream," one of the Chinese men holding her said. "Her kind always scream."

Jasmine clawed at the speaker, her fingernails scraping down his face, bringing blood.

"Bitch!" He swung at her but she ducked away.

Jasmine hadn't recovered from the shock yet. They had actually kidnapped her in plain sight right on Broadway! Terrible. She gulped down her fear, tried to quash all of the stories she had heard about Chinese girls vanishing and never being heard of again, and stared at the closest man.

"What are you doing?" she demanded.

"Giving you a ride, sweet little thing."

"You're kidnapping me. Nobody has any money to pay for me. You're making a mistake."

"No mistake." His hand came out and caught her breast. She hit him in the face with her fist, a reflex from her growing-up years in a less than perfect neighborhood.

The man slapped her hard, slamming her against the seat.

"Hit me again and I'll tear off both your tits!" he roared. "All we have to do is pick you up; nobody said anything about what shape you had to be in."

Jasmine cowered in the far corner of the car. Pick her up? Who? Kidnap her? Not for ransom, surely. Why? She began to tremble. She knew her brother was doing something with the police—no, the federal narcotics people. Was someone mad at her for what he had done?

It didn't make sense. None of it made any sense at all. She watched and waited. The car turned downtown, like it was taking her home. Soon they were in Chinatown and she had small darts of electricity shivering through her body.

The car drove into an alley and stopped. She was pulled out roughly and pushed toward a door.

"No noise and no screaming or I'll break your leg!" one of the big men said.

She went into the room, then was pushed ahead along a hallway and up two flights of steps. There she was shoved into a room that had no windows. She spun around as the door closed behind her and locked.

For a moment she wanted to beat on the door and scream, but she knew that would do no good. Where was Buzz? He would know what to do. He said something about working with her brother and helping with something to do with exposing some drug traffic.

Was that why she was here?

Before she could think further, the door opened and three men came into the room. Two stood next to the door and the other—taller, thin, with a smile—came forward.

"Jasmine, let me apologize for my workers. Sometimes they get a little overenthusiastic in their duties."

"Why was I kidnapped?" Jasmine shouted. She was surprised at the anger that crept into her words despite her fright.

"No, no. I merely wanted to talk to you. I know your brother, David Wong. He said he talked to you about his work. I only wanted to know what he told you."

"About what work, at the bank? That's all confidential. We don't talk about that."

"No, about some work he was doing with a friend, a Mr. Edwards, I think his name was."

"Edwards? He never mentioned the name. We have dinner together once a week. I have my own apartment downtown."

"Did he mention what he was doing with the federal people?"

"He said something about it. I think he was helping some federal drug people on a case. That's all he told me."

"Jasmine, are you telling me the truth?" He loomed over her, his Oriental features suddenly angry.

"Yes, yes I am. Now I demand that you let me out of here right now or I'll charge you with kidnapping. Right now!"

"I'm afraid that's impossible. Your brother said he told you everything."

She watched the man, calmer now. This person could be dangerous. He must be part of the drug establishment that David was helping the federal people with. She would be more careful.

"If he said that, it was because he thought you wanted him to say it. Did you beat him?"

"Yes, and we shall beat you too, and strip you naked and let my men play with you. I don't think you'd like that, Jasmine."

For a moment she felt chilled right down to her soul. She had tried to call David that morning. He hadn't been home before work when he should have been. At work they said he hadn't come in. She knew. They had killed her brother.

"I'll be glad to tell you again. My brother worked now and then with a friend, a Caucasian who I think worked for some federal drug agency. I don't know what he did, or when. He told me it was better that I didn't know. Why did you kill my brother?"

"Because he was hurting us, or you were, or someone was. He was available."

"So now you'll kill me because you could kidnap me? I don't know who you are, but you don't look that stupid. Are you?"

He slapped her. She swayed but stood there.

"My God, maybe you are," she said.

He slapped her again. Her foot rammed out in a quick dancer's kick, hitting his crotch but not with crushing force. The jolting of her soft shoe into his testicles brought a scream of rage from Mister Chu and he doubled over in agony. The two Red Stick guards grabbed Jasmine.

When Mister Chu was able to stand erect again, he

motioned with his hand, and the guards dragged Jasmine out of the room and down a long hallway.

At least she knew joy for a few short days, Jasmine thought as she fought them. She knew for sure now that the tall, thin man must be the leader of the drug syndicate and right now she was as good as dead.

Lin Liu sat in the delicious bath and for a moment luxuriated in it. It had been months since she'd had a bubble bath. For a moment she let herself revel in the pleasure, then slowly, her drug-filled mind came up with the facts.

She was being prepared. The same way they had done four years ago. She was getting a bath, she would get fine dresses and then a beautiful gown. She would be given carefully measured doses of mainlined heroin to keep her at the right response level.

A woman came into the large bathroom. Lin had never seen her before.

"Go away," Lin said.

The woman ignored her. She let the water out of the tub, attached a small spray tube and sprayed the bubbles off Lin, then dried her with a towel.

There was no way that Lin could protest other than a spoken word now and then. She felt as if she were wading through molasses. She could barely lift her hand. So well she remembered the ritual. The bath, the clothes, the shot, the suicide "letter," then the gown, chosen from among the most beautiful, expensive gowns she had ever seen. One would be picked out for her, and then they would take her to a room where the royal throne chair waited.

Lin screamed and bolted a step toward the woman, knocking her down. Lin tried to run to the door. But she could only move at a slow walk. Her mind raced ahead of her. She was ten feet from the door. Two women hurried in, grabbed Lin's naked form, and held her while another woman finished drying her, slipped a robe on her, and led her down a hall to another room.

She had made her try and failed. They would give her another shot soon. She had seen the process three times. It was a ritual that a winner would never forget.

"The dress is not right. It is too large for her," a woman said, and threw it at another woman there.

"Pin it up, sew it," the response came. "We have no time to make up a new one. It will not matter this time; there will be no winner."

They quieted their voices now as Lin looked at them.

Two Red Sticks held her as someone put a brown rubber tube around her arm so her vein would pop up and be easy to hit with the needle.

"No!" Lin shouted. In her mind she shouted it. By the time the signals got to her vocal cords and her mouth, they had weakened so much the word came out as a hushed whisper.

"No! I don't need any more!" Again the soft-spoken words of an old woman.

The young woman who used the needle did it neatly, with a quick stroke, and expertly shot the glory juice into her vein.

"If you give her too much and she can't sit up in the chair, you'll take her place," one of the Red Sticks snapped.

"I know my job," the girl said. "Both of you, get out of here."

The Red Sticks left and the woman finished dressing Lin, then applied makeup and did her hair. When the blower turned off and the hairdresser finished combing her out, Lin knew that it was over. Deeply in her subconscious the truth came through that she was not dead already because the New Control leaders had come up with a new way to utilize a traitor.

Put her in the chair and let her entertain the high rollers. Tears began to seep down her cheeks.

"No crying!" a voice shouted. "You just ruined a half-hour's makeup job!"

Lin looked at her and tried to laugh, but her laugh wasn't working. Lin thought of the gag line. If she ruined the makeup again she would *really* get into trouble. Her laugh still didn't work.

"How much time we got?" a voice asked.

"Relax, we did have two hours, but word just came down. They'll use the other girl, Ti her name was, tonight. This one will wait until tomorrow afternoon. So don't worry about her makeup. This is just a practice run."

"She'll be more than ready by then."

This time Lin laughed but only inside. She would not go on tonight; she had until tomorrow afternoon. It took her a while to understand the words. Then she laughed again, inside. She was going into hysterics but nobody knew it. She sat in the chair with a woman gluing long painted fingernails on her, another redoing her makeup, and a third doing a small change in her hairstyle. Then she understood. Ti would be the one to go on the throne chair tonight. Poor Ti! But there was nothing Lin could do to save her friend.

"Stand her up; I still need to fix that damn gown. I don't see why you picked this big, floppy one."

"Because at least half of her boobs have to show, you know that. Don't worry about it. It's coming off her now until tomorrow. We have lots of time."

Lin Liu heard it all. She was not sure that she believed it. They hadn't said much at all before, when she had been here four years ago. None of these women had been here then. It would be a job with a big turnover.

She wondered if Mister Chu was sure she was the traitor, or if he would kill all three of them to be sure. He would kill all of them. Maybe Matt would get there in time to save her. Sure, sure. She hadn't even told him where the headquarters were or where the high stakes Russian roulette game was played.

"Own damn fault," she said. The words never reached the outside world of the room.

Lin Liu sat there, drugged and beautiful. She knew the routine but had no idea if she would be able even to hold the pistol, let alone pull the trigger. A solitary tear squeezed out of her right eye and traced a line down her just-made-up cheek.

"Oh, damn!" the makeup woman said.

It was after ten o'clock that night that Hawke phoned Buzz at his apartment near the park.

"Yeah?"

"Buzz, Hawke."

"Christ! Where the hell you been? I been waiting for a call. Jasmine is gone, missing! She didn't show up for the rehearsal with a new girl this afternoon. She didn't come to the performance tonight. She didn't phone in to anyone. The girls she rooms with say that she left as usual for the rehearsal. Chu must have snatched her."

"Slow down, Buzz. Calm down. We don't know that for sure. Think it through. Chu might know about Jasmine from the newspaper story. If he did whack her brother, he might think David had told Jasmine something about him. Might have!"

"Yeah, might, and most damn well did. Now what do we do to get her back?"

"We don't have a prayer. We don't know where his operation is, where he works from."

Buzz screamed into the phone. "So ask the DEA. They must have some idea."

Hawke felt the WP grenade start to grow in his belly. It was not a good sign. "I'll call Frank right now and be back to you in ten minutes. Get ready to motor, your grungy working clothes. We won't be going first class. Bye."

He hung up and dialed Frank Edwards. It rang three times before Frank picked it up.

"Yeah, I'm on a stakeout. What?"

"Hawke. I think Chu snatched Jasmine, Wong's sister. I need to know Chu's headquarters, or somewhere that I can get a line on it. You have any addresses at all?"

"Jasmine? That little dancer? Christ, she's good. We don't know for sure, but we have a couple of leads." He rattled off what were at least banks and distributor points for heroin. "One in Harlem and the other in Queens. Take them both down if you want to. When I get back to the office at daylight, I'll dig up two more for you. We can have a regular war going down out there."

"Buzz is ready to use an atom bomb on Chinatown just to get Chu."

"Don't blame him. Cool it, I got to move. Bye."

The line went dead.

Hawke called Buzz again. "Harlem and Queens. I'll meet you in front of your building for a Harlem push. Take me a half hour to get up there."

"I'm ready. I'm using the Spas-12. It'll kill more damned druggers that way. If they hurt Jasmine, I'm not sure how much hell I'm gonna raise or how many druggers I'm gonna snuff. It'll make My Lai look like a church picnic!"

"I'm moving."

Hawke took his weapons suitcase and hurried down the elevator, then out to his car. One hubcap had been stolen. How would they sell just one? He drove as legally as he felt he needed to up Fifth Avenue and angled over to Buzz's place. As Hawke pulled up in front, Buzz emerged from some shrubbery and climbed in.

His face was frozen in a mask of anger. Hawke hadn't seen him that way since the day in 'Nam when things went to hell.

"Move it!" Buzz brayed. "Ain't got all fucking night!"

"We may need it. This place is probably a bank and distributor for pushers. But there just might be a phone number or an address. We also might get something from one of the house men. Keep hoping.''

They came off One Hundred Twenty-fourth at Windsor, rolled down a block, then parked in an alley. The target was a small grocery store that stayed open late for the convenience of the pushers, not for that of any customers. The grocery had a back door.

"This ain't my territory," Buzz said, looking out at a pair of black girls walking by.

"Some of your blood brothers will be inside with their hands in the till," Hawke snorted. Buzz held the Spas-12 and its nine rounds of double-aught buck ready to go. He had the Beretta 93-R stuffed in his belt and had one WP and one fragger grenade in his pockets.

Hawke carried the unsilenced Uzi and two blocks of C-3 with detonators and his .45 without the silencer in his belt. They went to the back door second over in the alley. It was locked. Hawke kicked it in, splintering a chain lock off the door frame up high. Three men lay passed out on the storeroom floor in alcoholic or drug stupors.

Hawke moved past them to a connecting door and listened through it. He could hear little. When he tried the knob he found it unlocked. Hawke looked at Buzz. "You take the left half of the room. Cover everyone there. Let's talk first unless we have to fire. We need information first, blood second.''

The door opened inward. Hawke pushed it hard and they slammed through back to back, sideways, each covering half the room. Lights were on. It was a meeting room with a dozen chairs, couches around the sides.

Only two men were inside, both Chinese. One lifted his hands when he saw the shotgun. The second man dove for a gun lying on a table beside a cardboard box.

He was Hawke's. The Uzi rattled a four-round burst, stitching the reaching hand against the owner's chest, where that slug and three more drilled through human bone and tissue and several vital centers. The hot lead slammed the man off the table and dead against the wall.

"Christ's sakes, my hands are up!" the other man screeched. "Don't kill me!"

"Anybody out front?" Hawke demanded.

"No, closed for the night. Just us two."

Hawke moved up to the small, rotund man and drove the heavy side of the eight-pound Uzi into his stomach. He bellowed in pain and doubled up on the floor. Hawke's toe touched his side, and he groaned and got up to his knees, then at last to his feet.

"You work for Mister Chu?"

He nodded.

"My friend here is going to put his shotgun against your chest. I'm going to count to five. If I get to five and you don't answer the question I give you, he'll pull the trigger. Have you ever seen a body when a round of double-aught buck hits it up close?"

The fat little man almost fainted. He shook so hard his teeth chattered. Twice he almost fell down.

"What . . . what question?"

"Where is Mister Chu's headquarters in Chinatown? I want the exact street address, the name of the building. Do you understand the question?"

The drugger nodded.

"Good. One."

Buzz pushed the Spas against the man's chest over his heart. The little man's eyes widened. He shivered.

"I'd be dead if I told you."

"If you don't, you're also dead, only quicker. Two."

He swallowed. His eyes glanced around the room, trying to find a way out. There was none. No way to beat a shotgun.

"The address!" Hawke roared in the man's face. "Three!"

"Look I'm just small stuff; you want the big ones. Go after them. Give me a chance!"

"Four!"

"All right! It's on Willow just off Mott aways."

"The address, the number," Hawke said softly.

The small man shook his head and closed his eyes.

Hawke slammed the side of the Uzi against the man's head, powering him over sideways to the floor and knocking him out.

"I wondered," Buzz said. "Knew we couldn't get anything out of him dead."

"Check around. We'll talk to him when he wakes up." Hawke handed Buzz a plastic riot cuff. "Hands," he said. Hawke put one on the man's ankles, binding them together.

They searched the room for twenty minutes, found two cardboard beer boxes filled with cash, thirty or forty one-pop-size packets of heroin, and a list of pushers with phone numbers. Nowhere did they find any other phone numbers or addresses.

Buzz looked at the pushers' list and scowled. "Most of these numbers are up here in Harlem. But two of them are from the Chinatown area. I know the prefixes."

"Write them down. We'll ask Frank's help."

The small man with the round belly had come back to this world a few minutes before but had kept quiet. Hawke touched his boot to the man's groin. He sat up.

"How's your memory? Did a broken jaw help?"

Now he wouldn't talk at all. Buzz started to kick him in the crotch, then decided against it.

"We about done here?" Buzz asked.

"Except for the garbage." Hawke stood over the drug distributor and snorted. "Little friend, when you deal in drugs, it's as dirty as you can get. You deal, you're dead. Ever wonder how many kids you've hooked, how many young girls you've put on their backs to feed their habit? How many people you've killed with this shit?"

Hawke shot him once in the forehead.

They picked up the boxes of drug money and went to the

door. Buzz took the WP out of his pocket. Hawke gave him a thumbs up. Buzz pulled the safety pin, let the handle flip off, and tossed the fire grenade into the meeting room.

They pulled the three winos out of the back room and stashed them in the alley away from where the fire would be. They were still in the alley when the grenade went off. By the time they were in the car and half a block down, the grocery store and drug distributing point burned brightly behind them.

They drove out of Harlem and halfway down the side of Central Park before Hawke pulled in at a phone.

Frank picked up the call on the second ring.

"Yeah?"

"Frank, I have two phone numbers; can you give me addresses on them?"

"In about two minutes."

Hawke told him the numbers and waited. When the addresses came, Hawke wrote them down. Neither one was on Willow or Mott street.

"We read some pusher lists up in Harlem, but the guy must have been trying to be cute. The phone numbers must be coded some way. We'll check them out, but it doesn't look good."

"You going to Queens?"

"No. Probably the same results. I think we'll tour Chinatown at night and through to the morning. Sometimes the night people know more about an area than day folks."

"True. I'm bunking in the office tonight if you want me. Otherwise I'll be working again in the morning. Good hunting."

Buzz didn't comment. He was boiling. Just below the surface he was a volcano ready to erupt. Hawke knew they had to find Jasmine quickly or Chinatown might soon cease to exist if Buzz took it on with his shotgun.

They drove past the first address. It was a block over from Willow, a store of Chinese art. Looked legitimate. The address of the second phone number was three blocks from Mott, a small herb store. It looked like an ideal front for something but could not be the headquarters for an organization as big as the New Control.

"So what the hell we do now?" Buzz asked. "This isn't helping us find Jasmine or Lin."

"We have to go with what we've got. An old newspaper saying about checking facts and waiting for developments. All we have is all we have."

"Golden Dragon isn't the kind of place for a corporate type office that Chu must have. But we might find something there," Buzz suggested.

"They know both of us by now. We wouldn't get past the front door."

"You sure Lin didn't give you some hint, some clue that would help us?"

"I've been over that night a million times. She said there was a girl she wanted to help before we charged into the place. She deliberately didn't tell me where the headquarters was."

"Great! So we sit around out here and they die within a mile or two of us and we can't do a fucking thing about it."

"I thought about that place I followed Lin back to after that first meeting that night—might be a clue. But we staked it out the next morning in our street bum duds and found that nothing went on there. At least no more people went in and out."

"So we've got nothing. If it was my call I'd go in the back door of the Golden Dragon, shoot up the place, and see where the rats ran for help. It might just work."

"Might. But half the people who work there are innocents trying to make a living cooking and washing dishes and waiting on tables. We owe them something, too."

"Dammit, Hawke, I'm not interested in logic or goodwill or being a nice guy. I want to stop Chu from killing the woman I'm going to marry."

"Why didn't you say so? Let's get out of the wheels and hunt for some night people who might know more than they think they do. Leave the Spas here. We'll go out with the handguns only. Let's start tipping over some garbage cans!"

CHAPTER
ELEVEN

The streets of Chinatown seemed darker than the rest of Manhattan, Hawke decided as they walked down a litter strewn alley, kicked past three sleeping forms, and watched for anything unusual.

The darkness might be because some of the streets were narrower, the lighting standards perhaps not as frequent, the shops and stores all having a distinctive foreign flavor.

"Place is like a tomb," Buzz said. "Where's all the gambling action I hear about down here?"

They found a wandering rag picker, a little old woman in her sixties with a grocery shopping cart piled with all of her worldly goods. She snarled at them, thinking they were competition. Buzz talked to her a few minutes in Mandarin, but he learned nothing.

"She tried to talk me out of my shirt," Buzz said. "She's never heard of any New Control, but she knows about the Red Sticks. Seems everyone in Chinatown has felt their wrath."

They sat in an alley mouth just off Mott Street and watched the small city-within-a-city as it pounded out its heartbeat. By then it was slightly after midnight. A few of the restaurants were still open. Up the street they could see the nightclubs flourishing, but here in the heart of Chinatown all seemed to be quiet.

There were few night people wandering around.

"We haven't even seen an opium den or a heavy betting parlor," Buzz said. "I've heard about them all my life but never seen one. My parents were squares, my old man a doctor. I was supposed to chop up hearts like he did, but I didn't enjoy all the blood."

"It's here somewhere," Hawke said. "All we have to do is find it."

"There's a pusher three doors down," Buzz said.

"Let's nail him and make him talk."

They sauntered onto the street. One of them kept the pusher in his sights as they wandered in that direction. He was short and well dressed. He wouldn't be armed—too big a risk. But he would have a stash nearby with the rest of his goods. They watched him leave the man he was talking to, fade back to the alley darkness, and vanish for a moment.

Then he was back, watching the street.

"Now," Hawke said quietly. They were within ten feet of the little man. They both charged him, picked him up, and vanished into the darkness of the alley mouth with him before he could do more than yelp in surprise.

They dropped him next to a wooden wall. Buzz searched him expertly and came up with a knife and two papers of heroin. They were simply slick magazine pages, torn into three-inch squares and folded over to hold a pop of heroin. They were easy to drop or could easily permit the joy juice to scatter on the sidewalk or alley if danger threatened.

"Two papers," Hawke growled at him. "Where's your stash?"

"No stash. That's it," the man shouted. "For you, twenty bucks each."

Buzz slapped him, snapping his head to one side.

"Your stash, now!" Buzz said, pressing the knife against the man's throat. "Your stash or you've got no throat left."

"Yeah, yeah. Okay. Over there." He pointed to the other side of the alley. When both looked that way he jerked away and ran down the alley. Hawke had him in ten steps, tripped him into the remains of a hundred Chinese dinners that had been scattered from a trash barrel by dogs.

Hawke put his foot on the man's throat.

"Mister Chu. I want his headquarters address. Don't worry, I'm not a cop. I'll cut you into slices of raw meat if you don't tell me."

"Hell, nobody knows. I'm way down on the ladder. I don't even know where my dealer works. I meet him here in the alley."

Hawke looked at Buzz, who nodded his agreement

"They get real cute down here."

"Get up!" Hawke ordered. The man scrambled to his feet and stood between Buzz and Hawke.

"Usually I shoot punks like you. This time I don't want to waste a bullet." Hawke took the man's arm, held it by the wrist with one hand and the elbow with the other. Then, before the pusher knew what was going down, Hawke lifted his leg and slammed the pusher's forearm down across his knee.

Both lower arm bones broke with a crack they all heard.

The pusher screeched in pain. "Bastard! You broke my fucking arm."

"So sue me," Hawke said, and he and Buzz walked out of the alley.

"Tighter than a snare drum head," Buss complained.

By 2:00 A.M. they had picked up no leads. They walked back to the car and took turns sleeping two hours at a time. At 6:00 A.M. they called Frank Edwards.

"You guys always get up this early?" a sleepy Frank asked.

"Usually. We've been working the night folks but didn't get much. Anything new?"

"Might be. Last night when you called, I transposed two of those numbers. I've got a new address for you, 593 Johnson. Might be worth checking out."

"Right, we're moving." Hawke told Buzz the address. It wasn't far away. As they turned into Johnson and drove along, both swore.

"Christ, this is where we spent half a day staking out the place!" Buzz yelled.

Hawke double-checked the numbers. "The 593 address is right beside the place where Lin went in that night. It's the damn Palace of Radiance and Beauty!"

"We know the place is dirty—let's crash in right now before they wake up," Buzz said.

"But we don't know how dirty. It could be just a cutting room. You have any contacts with the city or here in Chinatown that could give us any information about the place?"

Buzz shook his head. "Most city employees don't play the stock market."

They had driven past the block now and parked half a street farther down.

"The alley—let's take a look," Hawke said.

The alley here was narrow and dank. Buildings crowded back into it as if begrudging it the pass through space that was wide enough for only one car or small truck.

The fourth door in was for the Palace. It was locked from the inside, and there was no call button or light. They went through the alley to the next street but found no one, nothing that might furnish them with a clue.

Back in the car, they drove around the block and parked where they could see both the buildings. The Palace was smaller, only four stories with windows on the front looking like an old office building from the thirties.

Beside it sat the six story building that took up three

times the street frontage as the smaller one. It was newer, stone and brick construction, and appeared to be of much more recent origin. That was the one where Lin Liu had gone the first night they met her.

"Let's go in, hit them while they're still in their sacks."

Hawke watched Buzz a moment, then shook his head. "Can't risk it. They might be mostly civilians. We've got to be sure. We have to go in soft, then see what develops. To do that we have to wait until they open, or somewhere around normal business hours."

"Jasmine could be dead by then."

"True, so could Lin, but it's the best way to play it. We're still flying blind here. We have two positive leads from this area. Let's not blow it. We need more intel, but G-2 isn't helping us much. We wait."

"Damn!"

"Besides, on this mission I outrank you."

"Yes sir, Colonel, sir," Buzz said. It broke the tension and they sat in the car waiting. A corner shop opened and Buzz went for coffee and rolls for them. When he came back he looked at Hawke.

"Nothing has moved in or out of either building. I'd guess most activity takes place through other entrances, in back maybe. There must be people in there by now."

Inside the Palace of Radiance and Beauty the women were arriving for work. Most of them had jobs in the beauty salon that offered services for hair, nails, and facials. Some worked in a small spa with hot tubs and exercise machines and a large exercise room for aerobics.

Three rooms were reserved for special clients. In one of these Lin was just coming awake. She looked around, remembered the room with total revulsion, but knew there was nothing she could do about it.

The woman with the rubber tube and syringe came in with the two Red Stick guards. They held her the same way, but just before the woman injected the heroin into Lin's vein, another woman came in.

"Better change the dose. She's going into the throne room at ten o'clock, a special command performance for Mister Chu and selected high rollers."

The woman with the needle paused, made some mental calculations and shot half of the fluid down the sink. Then she put the rubber tube around Lin's arm and gave her the shot.

Lin screamed at them before the joy juice jetted into her bloodstream. Then as it powered through her system, she quieted and began to sing a song she hadn't thought of since childhood.

Hell, it might not be so bad. She'd won three times before. Maybe she'd win this time. She shrugged. Lin knew it was the heroin that calmed her, that turned her brain into mush, but there was not one damn thing she could do about it.

She watched the women come in. They would do her hair and nails again, and then, lastly, the makeup and the gorgeous gown. She loved to wear the gown. One of the women said the last one she wore was worth over a hundred thousand dollars.

Lin Liu watched the women dressing her and she kept singing the little song. She didn't even know what it meant now.

Just down the hall, Jasmine Wong had been given a much starker room. She still had her clothes, and she had a small bed and a sink. That was it. She had not slept at all last night. She lay awake staring at a light that she could not turn off.

What in the world did they want her for? She could not help them There could be no ransom, especially since they must have killed poor David. Tears stung her eyes. She wept just thinking about David. He had blundered in somewhere that was too deep for him and had been overwhelmed by the tong, or the triad, or whatever the evil ones were called now.

Jasmine sighed, then lay on her bed and cried, and at last she slept.

The two men in the rented car began to suit up. They each had their floppy shirts to conceal the weapons. Hawke had the Uzi with silencer under his shirt and a right-angled dual magazine that would hold sixty rounds of .45. He had the silenced .45 autoloader in his belt. His would be the silent attack.

Buzz slung the eight-pound Spas-12 by a cord around his neck. He had a pocket filled with sixteen double-aught buck shotgun shells. The Beretta would be in his hand, and four extra magazines of twenty rounds each rested in a big front pocket. He had a small shoulder bag that held the C-3 and detonators, as well as the six fraggers they hadn't used yet.

Both wore hats. Hawke had the floppy one he pulled low over his eyes. Buzz had on a khaki fatigue cap that looked like he had worn it for fifty missions in 'Nam.

"Ready?" Hawke asked.

"Ready for Freddy—you remember that one?"

Mister Chu sat up in his king-size bed with satin sheets and stared at the two girls beside him. Both were fourteen. He had selected them carefully. When they were seventeen they would be moved to new work and he would have the joy of making a new selection. Mister Chu thought about that. Well, he might wait only until they were both fifteen.

He kicked out of the sheet and walked nude to the bathroom. After his shower he ate breakfast in his sixth floor apartment overlooking a slice of Manhattan. Soon he wanted a bigger building, a tall one with a good view. He was tired of looking at the underbelly of this town.

Yen Kao came in and laid out the day's schedule.

"First thing at ten will be the throne room, where some

entertainment is planned for you and two dozen high rollers. Results are guaranteed.''

"Ah, yes, Lin. A shame, really. A talented girl. But once the apple goes rotten, it must be thrown out quickly.''

"After that we'll do a tour of the outlets in Queens. We also have an emergency meeting with our procurement section. The three lost shipments must be replaced within a week. It will mean special arrangements by air.''

"Yes. Don't remind me. But it must be done.''

"Oh, we lost a distributor in Harlem last night. Much the same type attack as before. Both distributors dead, the store burned to the ground, and arson squads and police all over the place finding our goods. Hell to pay up there.''

"Enough! I want some good news for a change. How long to the fun and games downstairs?''

"About an hour, Mister Chu.''

"Bring me the newspapers and come back five minutes before show time.''

Hawke and Buzz went up to the street level door of the Palace of Radiance and Beauty. They had seen three Chinese women go in. All three looked like their hairdos needed an overhaul. Buzz took the lead.

The women had not knocked, they simply opened the door and went in. Buzz and Hawke did the same thing, playing it cool and soft.

Inside they found a reception area, a room about twenty feet square with a variety of chairs and upholstered furniture around the walls. A receptionist at the small desk smiled at them and said something in his native tongue to Buzz.

"No, I'm afraid you're mistaken,'' Buzz said in English. "We're here to see Mister Chu and to blast him directly into hell.''

As soon as he said it two Red Sticks stepped into the room with their batons.

Hawke pulled out the Uzi and Buzz lifted the Spas-12.

The guards panicked and darted through a curtain. Buzz and Hawke rushed after them. The Red Sticks took exactly the wrong action: they ran to their strength, to help.

They scurried down a flight of steps, past a long hallway, and down more steps. They came to a room where six Red Sticks lifted their batons, and one pulled a .38 revolver. Hawke chattered out a dozen silent rounds from the Uzi, and Buzz triggered a single round from the Spas. The six Red Sticks dissolved into bleeding, groaning rubble on the floor.

Hawke kicked open a door they had been protecting. He found another set of steps that went down, then a long hallway. At the end of the hall he and Buzz saw a more elaborate door.

He eased it open and at almost the same instant he heard a shot boom out from the room just ahead. He kicked open the door, saw Lin Liu sitting on a golden throne chair on a long polished table with two dozen cheering, shouting older Chinese men around it.

No one looked in their direction.

Hawke saw Lin sitting in the throne chair, the revolver frozen in her right hand, her body fallen against the side of the elaborate chair, and her face stilled in death.

"Not again!" Hawke screamed. The men turned to look at him. He fired six bursts of six or seven rounds each from the Uzi. Bodies dropped and rolled, men screamed. A few fell to the floor and crawled behind the big table.

Buzz fired three times into the melee, watching the heavy double-aught slugs chop up flesh, drive eyeballs out of sockets, tear torsos in half and chop up the dead and dying.

"Enough!" Hawke bellowed. "Don't anyone move or you're dead. Are there more girls to be sacrificed?"

One man with a bleeding right arm looked up.

"Out the doors, one flight up," then he fainted.

Hawke and Buzz charged through the small door the man had pointed to, rushed up the steps and found a hallway.

There were six rooms off it. The first was locked. Hawke smashed the lock open with a vicious kick. The room was empty.

In the fourth room they found Jasmine. She looked at them coyly, then giggled. She wore a beautiful gown with gold braid and a long skirt that swept the floor. Her hair was beautifully set on top of her head and her face professionally made up.

Buzz ran forward, caught her in his arms.

"Should I know you?" she asked softly.

"Drugged," Buzz said. "The bastards!"

"Out, tactical withdrawal," Hawke snapped. "The alley. There has to be an alley. Can you carry her?" Buzz nodded and swept her out of the chair.

Hawke swung the Uzi around. He had already pushed in the other end of the L-shaped magazine. In the hall he saw two Red Stick guards. One four-round burst cut them down and they moved in that direction. He figured they were still two floors below ground level. The next stairway they found they rushed up.

Buzz carried Jasmine effortlessly. At the top of the stairs, Hawke paused. He saw no one. Then two men stepped out of a doorway with pistols. Hawke sent four silenced rounds at them, then four more.

They ran to the stairs the men had protected and charged up, then down a short hallway to the alley door. They slipped outside and slammed the barrier.

"Down to the street and grab a taxi. Take her to your place. I'll meet you there. First, give me the scatter gun and your ammo. I've got a date with Mister Chu." Hawke slung the weapon on the cord around his neck and pushed ten more shotgun shells into his pockets. He put in new loads until the shotgun was filled with nine rounds. Then he checked his Uzi. He had about ten rounds left in it and another thirty-round magazine. Enough. He caught the bag of C-3 explosives and grenades from Buzz, then waved him off.

Hawke watched Buzz until he was out of the alley, then he ran back into the doorway and searched for someone alive. He found a woman near a wounded man.

Slowly he lifted the Ingram. "Tell me where Mister Chu's offices are or you're dead."

"Yes! Don't shoot. Up the stairs to the fourth floor. Connecting door into the next building. Mister Chu's offices on top floor, six."

Hawke pushed the woman to one side and ran upward. He found two gunmen on the second floor and wasted them with a ten-round burst that ran the Uzi dry. He dropped the L magazine and pushed in a new thirty-rounder and moved up to the third floor.

Five men with guns had upended a heavy desk in the hallway, blocking his way. He sent one round of double-aught buck around the side of the desk and heard a scream of pain.

Then he dug out a fragger and flipped it toward the desk. It went too far down the hallway, exploding with a shattering roar, but did little damage to the defenders. The second grenade landed just behind the desk. Someone tried to grab the bomb and throw it back. But that happens only in the movies—4.2 seconds isn't long enough to make a forward pass.

The grenade went off and Hawke spurted down the hall, sent a burst into two Chinese Red Sticks still moving behind the desk, then charged on up to the fourth floor.

Only two Red Sticks with their batons challenged him. Hawke laughed and shot both, then saw the connecting doorway. He pushed it open and let it swing back, jumping against the solid wall.

A blast of a dozen guns sounded and the door splintered in several places. Hawke dug out another grenade, pushed the door with his Uzi and rolled the grenade inside.

He heard screams before the bomb exploded, then the roar of the grenade knocked one door off its hinges. Hawke drove through the other door with the Spas-12 up and ready. Three men to the far side staggered up and lifted weapons.

One round of the double-aught buck shattered them backward in a spray of blood.

Ahead to the left was another stairway. He saw no defenses. Hawke surged up halfway and stopped. Two weapons fired from above, expecting him to continue. He dug out another grenade, pulled the safety pin, and held the arming handle. Slowly he edged upward. He saw an office setup. The fifth floor. Behind a desk he spotted two gunmen. He rolled the grenade under the desk. It stopped when it hit a brown pants leg and exploded in the gunman's lap.

One more floor. Hawke rammed through double doors and up the steps toward six. So far so good. He brought up the Spas-12 and watched. He heard movement above. He bent low and came up as before so he could see over the top of the last step.

As he did he saw ten Red Sticks running toward him. The Spas fired four times and the ten men flopped to the ground in various stages of agony and death.

Behind them he saw a door close slowly. He couldn't get to it before it shut with a metallic clunk. Hawke looked at the lock in the center next to the wall. He backed up and fired two rounds from the Spas-12. The thin metal and the doorjamb blew away with the hot lead, and the door swung open.

Someone fired a handgun twice, but Hawke was already standing against the wall and out of the line of the bullets. When he jumped in to fire, the figure was gone. He popped up on the other side of a heavy desk and fired the gun, a .45 auto. Hawke dove past the door into the hallway out of range.

"Who the hell *are you?*" a voice called from inside the room.

"An avenging angel who's here to collect from you. Are you Chu?"

There was no answer. Hawke lifted the Spas-12, lunged through the door, blasting one round as he went, and dove behind another desk over from the big one.

"Bastard!" someone crowed, then mewed in pain. "Money? You want money? I'll give you five million right now to put down your weapons and get out of here."

"Cheapskate!" Hawke threw a grenade at the spot where he thought the voice had come from. The fragger exploded with an ear-thumping roar. For a moment Hawke couldn't hear a thing.

A form rose from this side of the explosion, both hands over its ears. Hawke surged forward and clubbed him alongside the head with the side of the Spas-12, and he went down like a waterfall.

Hawke looked around the room checking the other areas, but they were the only two in the room.

He went back, lifted the unconscious man, and threw him in a big office chair, then slapped his face until he revived.

"What the hell?"

"Are you Dong Chu?" Hawke asked in a level, deadly voice.

"Yeah, yeah. Who are..." He stopped. Chu's mind cleared and he knew where he was, what had happened. "You fucking bastard!"

"Flattery won't work, Chu. I'm here to collect. I want a billion dollars in cash, right now, or your worthless life. One or the other."

"Who are you?"

"Name wouldn't mean a thing. Some people call me The Avenger."

"Oh, damn, heard of you... Your wife..."

"Right. Now I'm going to do the same thing to you." He

lifted the .45 from his belt and slammed a round into the floor beside Chu's foot.'

"Oh, Christ!"

"Talk. Your people killed David Wong and Lin Liu?"

"Yes. Had to be done. Security."

"You've been picking up addicts off the street and using them in your Russian roulette gambling games?"

"They were down and dead anyway... no loss!"

Hawke shot him through the right foot. Chu keened in pain and at last screamed in his rage. When he quieted, Hawke slapped him hard across the face.

"You kidnapped Jasmine Wong?"

"Yes. Didn't hurt her."

"Only because we arrived in time."

Hawke pulled out desk drawers. "I want a list of everyone who works for you, all of your operations, computer reports."

"Don't have any."

Hawke snorted, pulled out another drawer, and saw the printouts of the total operation. Lin Liu had won after all. The reports listed personnel, home addresses and phone numbers, duties, points of operation, everything.

Hawke tied Chu's hands behind him with another plastic riot cuff from his deep pocket.

Then he took our a grenade and pulled the safety pin.

"Know what this is, Chu?"

Chu's eyes went wide and he nodded.

"Good, it's your passport to hell." Chu's stare never left the grenade. "Say hello to everyone in hell for me, Chu. I won't be coming for a while yet."

He slapped Chu twice, and when the drug boss opened his mouth to scream, Hawke jammed half the grenade inside, then forced his jaws apart until the entire grenade was inside Chu's mouth. Only the handle, which Hawke held firmly to the body of the grenade, was outside the drug czar's mouth.

Hawke took his handkerchief and tied it around Chu's mouth under the arming handle, but kept the handle in place.

"Like I said, Chu, say hello to your buddies in hell!"

Hawke let go of the handle, which popped off, arming the weapon, and Hawke sprinted for the big doors. He dove past them to safety just as the grenade went off. When the shrapnel stopped buzzing, Hawke stepped back in the room.

Dong Chu would never be recognized. Fingerprints might identify him. His head had been shattered into half a dozen pieces and blown completely off his neck. Blood spattered the whole room.

Hawke checked the loads in his Spas-12, put in his last four rounds, and headed for the stairs. He doubted if anyone would stop him from going to the street.

No one did.

Two hours later, Hawke had dumped all of his weapons and explosives in the Hudson River, except for the silenced .45, which he could fly in his luggage. He had carried the suitcase, two boxes, and three sacks of cash up to Buzz's apartment and set them on a table.

"How is she?" Hawke asked.

"Better. She's almost out of the drugs. The first thing she wanted me to do was call the show and tell them she'd be back tomorrow night. I explained what had happened to the stage manager. I think I squared it all."

"Good." Hawke pointed at the cash. "Small problem. I need you to set up a trust for me. Deposit it nine thousand dollars at a time so no questions are asked. I want you to take a hundred thousand and invest it for Jasmine. In her name and under her complete control. Same amount goes to you for your assistance. I'll carry the suitcase with me on my travels. Put the rest in a trust in my name with your address, and reinvest the interest until I get in touch with you."

"We're talking about over two million in a trust?"

"Whatever it comes to. I trust you."

Hawke called Frank. He was in the New Control headquarters.

"Christ, what a mess," Frank said. "You guys don't spare the horses, do you? So far we've got dead bodies stacked up like cordwood. I also found those records you left for me in that big envelope with my name on it. Thanks. We can absolutely say that New Control is out of business, in all of its divisions."

"And you don't know how the hell it happened," Hawke prompted.

"Yeah, I don't know how the hell it happened, but I'm glad it did. Gonna be hell to pay over all the blood. Right now I'm talking up the theory that there was an internal power struggle. I think I can sell it. We found David Wong's body. I'm putting him in for a special medal. Giving him most of the credit for infiltrating the place. You find Jasmine?"

"Yes, she's safe."

"Good. I get a feeling I won't be seeing you again."

"True. I'm moving. Got a new job offer I can't refuse."

"Some unlucky son-of-a-bitch somewhere." They both laughed.

They said good-bye and Hawke phoned his double-blind number in San Diego. The first drop rang in Denver, which automatically forwarded the call to Seattle. There the signal was automatically forwarded from that number to the apartment facing Balboa Park in San Diego.

Someone lifted the receiver on the second ring.

"Hello."

"Linda Barlow, this is a friend of yours. How is everything?"

"Matt! So good to hear from you! Where are you? Are you all right? When are you coming home? I got a date for the junior prom. Isn't that absolutely rad! *Where are you?*"

"I'm ready to move. Any ideas?"

"Oh, yes. One of the biggest talent agents in Hollywood took out a half page ad in the *Union* newspaper here trying to find The Avenger. I went to a phone booth and called the agent. He says he has a big problem up in Hollywood with meth and coke and Mexican brown heroin. He says he needs your help desperately. I have his name and number."

"Yes, something to think about. I'm flying out there soon. Then we'll talk some more. How are your deposits coming along?"

"Fine, but the teller is getting a little curious."

"Hold off a while. Oh, about flying. I'm going to sleep the clock around and have two big steak dinners, then I'll be flying out. Keep things in check."

"I will. I miss you and want you to come home. So anytime you come, call me and I'll meet you at the airport."

Hawke said good-bye and hung up.

"We both better get some sleep," he said to Buzz. "I'll take this one suitcase and leave the rest in your hands. Frank said the cops have the New Control wiped out and he has all the records."

"Yeah, good. Now I can burn those fatigues. I've had enough of the fast and deadly lane for a long time. Besides, I have to square everything with Jasmine. I mean, I'll have responsibilities."

Hawke grinned and walked out the door with the suitcase filled with money. He'd stash it in San Diego.

For just a moment he thought about his wife Connie. Was his debt to her paid yet? Hell no. Right now it felt like he could never hurt the drug people enough to even the score.

He'd take on Hollywood. He'd dig into the drug traffic in the make-believe capital and see if he could strip down a little of the tinsel.

"Watch out Hollywood, you're next on my hit list," Hawke said softly.

America's weapon against global terrorism...

Cody's ARMY

They're top-secret warriors. An anti-terrorist guerrilla unit that's ready to strike anywhere, at a moment's notice, with direct orders from the President to get the job done...now matter how.

☐ CODY'S ARMY
(C30-212, $2.95, U.S.A.)
(C30-213, $3.95, Canada)

☐ CODY'S ARMY #4: Belfast Blintz
(C34-501, $2.95, U.S.A.)
(C34-502, $3.95, Canada)

☐ CODY'S ARMY #2: Asssault Into Libya
(C30-214, $2.95, U.S.A.)
(C30-215, $3.95, Canada)

☐ CODY'S ARMY #5: D.C. Firestrike
(C34-503, $2.95, U.S.A.)
(C34-504, $3.95, Canada)

☐ CODY'S ARMY #3: Philippine Hardpunch
(C30-216, $2.95, U.S.A.)
(C30-217, $3.95, Canada)

☐ CODY'S ARMY #6: Hellfire in Haiti
(C34-505, $2.95, U.S.A.)
(C34-506, $3.95, Canada)

Warner Books P.O. Box 690 New York, NY 10019

Please send me the books I have checked. I enclose a check or money order (not cash), plus 95¢ per order and 95¢ per copy to cover postage and handling.* (Allow 4-6 weeks for delivery.)

___Please send me your free mail order catalog. (If ordering only the catalog, include a large self-addressed, stamped envelope.)

Name _____

Address _____

City _____ State _____ Zip _____
*New York and California residents add applicable sales tax.   323